CARNIVAL

Also translated by Arunava Sinha

17 by Anita Agnihotri
A Ballad of Remittent Fever by Ashoke Mukhopadhyay
A Mirrored Life by Rabisankar Bal
Abandon by Sangeeta Bandyopadhyay
Black Rose by Buddhadeva Bose
Chowringhee by Sankar
Dozakhnama by Rabisankar Bal
Fever by Samaresh Basu
Illicit by Dibyendu Palit
Kabuliwallah by Rabindranath Tagore
Kalabati the Showstopper by Moti Nandy
Khauna-Mihir's Mound by Bani Basu
Kick-off: Stories from the Field by Moti Nandy
My Kind of Girl by Buddhadeva Bose
On A Truck, Alone To McMahon by Nabaneeta Dev Sen
Panty by Sangeeta Bandyopadhyay
Seven Heavens by Samim Ahmed
Shameless by Taslima Nasreen
Tagore for the 21st Century Reader
The Aunt Who Wouldn't Die by Sirshendu Mukhopadhyay
The Chieftain's Daughter by Bankimchandra Chattopadhyay
The Fifth Man by Bani Basu
The Magic Moonlight Flower and Other Enchanting Stories by Satyajit Ray
The Master and I by Soumitra Chatterjee
The Merry Tales of Harshabardhan and Gobardhan by Shibram Chakraborty
The Middleman by Sankar
The Murderer's Mother by Mahasweta Devi
The Rhythm of Riddles: Three Byomkesh Bakshi Mysteries by Saradindu Bandyopadhyay
The Sickle by Anita Agnihotri
There Was No One at the Bus-Stop by Sirshendu Mukhopadhyay
Three Women: Nashtaneer, Dui Bon, Malancha by Rabindranath Tagore
What Really Happened & Other Stories by Banaphool
When the Time Is Right by Buddhadeva Bose
Wonderworld and Other Stories by Sunil Gangopadhyay
You are Neera by Sunil Gangopadhyay

CARNIVAL

a novel

SAYAM BANDYOPADHYAY

Translated from the Bengali by
ARUNAVA SINHA

ALEPH BOOK COMPANY
An independent publishing firm
promoted by *Rupa Publications India*

Originally published in the Bengali as
Puranpurush by Dey's Publishing, Kolkata

First published in English in India in 2024
by Aleph Book Company
7/16 Ansari Road, Daryaganj
New Delhi 110 002

Copyright © Sayam Bandyopadhyay 2019
English translation copyright © Arunava Sinha 2024

All rights reserved.

This is a work of fiction. Names, characters, places, and incidents are either the product of the author's imagination or are used fictitiously and any resemblance to any actual persons, living or dead, events, or locales is entirely coincidental.

No part of this publication may be reproduced, transmitted, or stored in a retrieval system, in any form or by any means, without permission in writing from Aleph Book Company.

ISBN: 978-81-19635-50-4

1 3 5 7 9 10 8 6 4 2

Printed in India

This book is sold subject to the condition that it shall not, by way of trade or otherwise, be lent, resold, hired out, or otherwise circulated without the publisher's prior consent in any form of binding or cover other than that in which it is published.

In memory of my father

Contents

Invocation / vii

Part One

One / 3

Two / 11

Three / 39

Four / 44

Part Two

Five / 93

Six / 95

Seven / 144

Eight / 156

Notes / 158

Invocation

This is, first and last, a novel. It is not set, however, in the time we occupy. It goes back more than 150 years. But writing about history does not necessarily make a novel historical. Here history is merely a medium which is trying to tell the story of someone or the other from our own time, to say the things someone or the other has not said. The nature of words that remain behind a veil is the same in all eras. History, country, or language cannot create any differentiation. This novel seeks to surmise the future, it wants to anticipate human thinking and cogitation. Nineteen has infiltrated the body of twenty, or twenty has assimilated nineteen. In fact, all centuries are part of one another's bodies in this manner. None of us has a language of our own, nor an emotion. Each of us has, all of us have, borrowed one another's language, one another's emotions—consciously and unconsciously—over the centuries. What time has changed is expression, the manner of application. The rest is unchanged.

So, *Carnival* owes as much to Christopher Marlowe and Johann Wolfgang von Goethe as it does to Thomas Mann, Mikhail Bulgakov, and Klaus Mann.

It is indebted, too, to the city of Kolkata, being taken in every time by the ruse of a Mephistopheles to shed its character like a sloughing snake, always in search of an immense carnival.

PART ONE

'The mind is superior to the senses, intelligence superior to the mind, the soul superior to intelligence, even more superior to this great truth is the unsaid, that is, true nature.'

—Katha Upanishad

'Stories talk of nothing but the world that was.'

—Kamalkumar Majumdar

ONE

Rajaram was startled by the perfumed cold breeze filtering in through the raised window slats. He sat up with a start. Where had his senses been all this while? He had waited so long for this moment, prepared so hard for it—had it just passed him by? Had he fallen asleep despite all his expectations and anxieties? The very next moment he reassured himself—no, it wasn't sleep exactly, he had merely dozed off. It couldn't exactly be called slumber. He had merely been overtaken by a momentary drowsiness, inevitable since he had stayed up all night. And a chilly wind had taken this opportunity to steal in and occupy the room. It seemed to Rajaram as soon as he shook off his drowsiness that his body had been guarding against this draught like a sleepless sentry. After all, he hadn't felt cold. But now that he was alert, his body seemed to have relaxed its vigilance. He was feeling the chill. Moreover, because of his alertness, he could hear the whistling of the wind, he could even smell it. There was an iciness near his lips. Pushing out the tip of his tongue, he got an insipid taste. There was a frosty touch beneath his ears. Was it time, then? It was still dark outside. Dawn was about ninety minutes away. Glancing at the wall clock, Rajaram recollected Anadi Siddhantabagish's calculation. This was the appointed hour. The glow of the lamp was dimming; through the glass chimney, he could see the tip of the flame turning black.

Oh! Could I ever have imagined such a dawn were possible? That such a dawn would come? Can anyone stop me now? I am marching ahead. Leaving everything behind. Catch me. Catch me if you can. Tie me up. You cannot. Can you? You cannot. Look, I cannot keep my eyes open. They're closing. Am I going to sleep again? But no, this is not the sleep you are thinking of. In any event, I simply cannot sleep now. I must stop my eyes from closing. But will I be able to sleep ever again? Will I be able to indulge my eyes when they close? I do not know; I do not know. All I know is I am marching ahead; I am leaving everything behind. Stop me if you can. Stop me…look, I am alert.

His eyelids had returned to their appointed place. Both his eyes smarted a little. The breeze sent a tingle down the pores of his skin and up his phallus. Rajaram could tell that the sheet wrapped around his body had been displaced down to his thighs. Clamping his knees together, he traced the skin on his chest with his fingertips before pulling the sheet back up to cover his body. Everything had become far too chilly at the crack of dawn today. Or perhaps it was a regular feature in this season of rain, but on other days Rajaram was asleep at this hour with the window tightly latched. Today, though, he was awake, and it wouldn't do to keep the window closed. And so, the slats were tilted upwards, and the inner frame with the glass pane was open.

Perhaps it was because he was naked that he felt the assault of the cold all the more. His habit of sleeping in the nude, with only a sheet to cover his body, was twenty-one years old. He was forty-eight now. Propping the pillow up behind his back, Rajaram sat up again and leaned back against it. It was the same pose that he had maintained since midnight, till he had dozed off briefly and begun to droop.

Simantini was sleeping on the floor near the door, close to the wall. Her milk white fur looked bluish in the darkness, which was almost complete. Rajaram saw there was plenty of milk in her bowl. So, she had drunk only a little when it was given to her. He usually checked every day whether she had finished all her milk, but he had forgotten all about it today.

It occurred to him that when you were consumed by your own affairs you probably had no time to think of anyone else's.

Simantini was sleeping peacefully now. Her stomach swelled and then subsided as she inhaled and exhaled. He would have to wake her up when it was time. She was his only heir and living witness. And at once Rajaram reflected that he was thinking of himself again. Was there to be no respite from this?

He did not have the answer to this question. What he knew was that this was the time to wait. There was nothing to do but wait quietly. Rajaram tried to stare at the joists overhead without blinking. The valance of the fan suspended from the roof swayed repeatedly in the breeze. The heat was all but gone. The punkah puller had been granted a few days' leave with pay, although Rajaram knew full well that this leave was going to be permanent.

> Do you know I'm running away today, punkah puller? No, you don't. You have been given leave and are under the impression you will be back. As you have in the past. But this time you will be dumbfounded when you return. I am running away. Without telling anyone. Ask Simantini if you can. She is the only one who can

give you the correct information. All I remember is the way you look. Stout and stubby, with fleshy fingers and toes. You sweated when pulling on the punkah rope; in the glow of the sky at night those beads of perspiration looked like dewdrops. The sweat glistened on your dark skin. Your arms flexed above your elbows. I came out of the room often to look at you, but you never realized it. How old are you? What about your family? I have never got round to asking these questions. The fact is I am not much of a conversationalist, you know.

The room was suffused with the fragrance of ittar. The scent entered Rajaram's body with every breath, finding a passage through his nose, all the way to the inner chambers of his brain, and touching his senses. He felt a sudden sense of wonder—once an external essence had infiltrated the body, how was one to be free of it?

He didn't know. But Rajaram was delighted by his own query. Some questions take birth unexpectedly, apparently without a suitable answer, and yet have the power to entertain the questioner or the listener.

A long time ago, after lavishing considerable thought on the price (for though he was a landowner, he worried forever about unnecessary expenses), Rajaram had purchased a vial of ittar in Chitpur. Made from rose petals, it probably had something else—the extract of another flower—mixed into it. He was not aware of the manufacturing process, but he was curious about it. Even a dab made it as constant a companion as a shadow. After his bath, or before he went out, Rajaram put a spot of the ittar near each of his earlobes, on his shoulders, wrists, and both sides of the elbows. The fragrance spread slowly, seemingly exuded by his skin. Rajaram's spirits were lifted.

When will I use this ittar again? Should I take it with me?

Rajaram's eyelids continued to flutter. Sensing the extent and permanence of the fragrance in the room, he had the impression that his cherished vial of ittar had, despite his best efforts to keep it safe, fallen to the floor and smashed into pieces. It was the same scent, just like his own ittar.

The vial wasn't visible clearly in the darkness. But Rajaram resisted the urge to get out of bed and check. Turning his head, he fixed his eyes on the mirror. A little later, he realized the vial was intact. It had not fallen. Preserved with great care beside the mirror, the precious vial of ittar gave a hint of a metallic liquid in this semi-darkness. A stilled golden hue. Rajaram was relieved.

So it was the breeze that had borne into the room a fragrance similar to the one of this ittar's. But where had the breeze brought it from? What was the source of this scent? He wondered why he was being drawn to a mere vial of ittar in his final moments.

His body was touched constantly at different points by a stealthy excitation. Resting on his chest, the fingers of his left hand trembled every now and then. The words forced themselves out through his lips—

He severed the heads of Ravan, not one but ten.
But with the creator's boon they sprouted again.

A long time ago, without being observed, Rajaram had heard his father Debram reading Kashiram Das's Mahabharat. It was an evening made dolorous by rain. Debram was sitting alone on his bed, intoning the verses from the Kashidasi Mahabharat published by the Serampore Mission Press, which was open on his bookstand. He read it often, beginning where he had stopped last time. That day he was reading the section set in the forest.

A freshly adolescent Rajaram was on his way to his room when he heard his father's voice while passing his door. The verses he heard were Debram reading the Mahabharat. Curious to know which section of the Mahabharat it was, Rajaram had stopped close to the door, taking care that his shadow was not visible, in case his father stopped on seeing it. He listened raptly as Debram read, his voice quavering ever so slightly.

> He severed the heads of Ravan, not one but ten.
> But with the creator's boon they sprouted again.
> Every time he beheaded the villain with a cry,
> Past deeds did not let the evil Ravan die.

Debram continued reading, but Rajaram's mind had paused on the two lines: 'He severed the heads of Ravan, not one but ten, But with the creator's boon they sprouted again.' He was unmoved by what his father was reading or how far he had progressed. The words kept circling and tumbling in his head, 'The heads of Ravan, not one but ten....'

Why was he in this state? Rajaram could not discern the reason. Was it the cadence of the words or the rhythm of the poetry or the story of the renewal of Ravan's power? The true reason for this composition was unknown to him, but as is the case when one is startled, Rajaram registered nothing else. Only these words whirled in his mind and ear, as though he had not heard anything other than these, not even the next two lines.

Since then, he often uttered these two lines, in the form of a muttered soliloquy or loudly for the benefit of others, both consciously and without his own awareness. His listeners had not been able to do anything but express their surprise at their irrelevance. The couplet came to Rajaram's mind as he passed through a range of mental states. But what was common to every such occasion was the fact that it was always under the spell of climbing excitement. The words emerged from him at these times as naturally as breath, without self-control. Unknown to himself, an oral practice and passion in the guise of a supernatural chant was created, 'He severed the heads….'

∽

The occasional scratch of Simantini's claws betrayed her restlessness in her sleep. Maybe she was dreaming.

Rajaram remembered having a dream of his own during his brief spell of light sleep earlier. His last dream, perhaps….

An unknown city. Even if some of the places did look like the ones in the city he knew, the vehicles and their riders and all the buildings seemed bizarre. Such strange people! So many of them! And wearing peculiar garments of a kind Rajaram had never seen. Nor had he ever observed such a variety of coiffures, moustaches, and beards. Which period was this? None of the people looked at anyone else; they appeared oblivious to one another's existence. Or they were in denial of it. All of them were walking, but they also kept talking, with one of their hands, left or right, placed on the corresponding ear. They talked and they walked endlessly. Rajaram noticed in astonishment that the footprints they had left behind were smeared with blood…the road was covered in bloody footprints. But all of this was entirely natural here—no one gave it a second glance, they simply walked on with blood beneath their feet. Standing in a corner, Rajaram lifted his own right foot to examine the sole….

And that was when the dream snapped. Such extraordinary goings-on! Another unusual dream, just like before. And blood, again.

As he recollected this dream, Rajaram's excitation seemed to gather an enchanted momentum. He tried to mitigate his fervour without completing the line, 'He severed the heads….' His continence had to last only a little longer. After that, the ultimate carnival!

Rajaram slumped in his bed, turning on his side and closing his eyes. He yawned. And as soon he smelt the pillowcase, he recalled Krishnabhabini's bracelet.

TWO

Autumn was fading, and the advent of winter was increasingly evident in nature's changing ways. There was soft sunshine and a mild breeze during the day. At dusk, the leaves could often be heard falling. Occasional gusts of wind scattered them everywhere—this sound could be heard too. The darkness established its reign at night. The breeze became even fainter. A time of slackness.

It happened on a chilly night during this period. Krishnabhabini's death that night made Rajaram even colder.

~

When she went to serve Krishnabhabini her food that night, Shashi did not receive a response despite calling out several times. She felt apprehensive, for she didn't usually have to call her name so many times. One knock on the door was all it took for Krishnabhabini to open it with a smile and take her food. She even exchanged a few words usually. Was something the matter today?

The two windows of her room faced inwards. They looked out on what Rajaram grandly referred to in English as the 'inner courtyard'. Both were closed, and it was impossible to tell what was going on inside. Lifting the slats would not offer a clear view, since thick and opaque window panes lay beyond them. Besides, it probably wouldn't be appropriate to lift the slats just yet. Instead, Shashi flattened her ear against the door in search of sounds from within, her cheek and jaw coming into contact with the wood.

No, there was no sound to be heard.

Shashi now tried to peer through the opening at the bottom to check whether the lamp was lit. No, it was dark. No lights.

Had Krishnabhabini fallen asleep? It was far too early. Indisposed, then? Shashi pushed on the door again, this time with some force, and called out once more.

No response.

Shashi raced downstairs, the lamp in one hand and the plate of food in the other. She was panting. Latu had just returned after bringing Rajaram his dinner and was tidying the kitchen. Shashi informed him that the lights were out in Krishnabhabini's room, and she wasn't answering though Shashi had called out to her many times.

At first, Latu could not decide what to do. Fetch Rajaram or take a look for himself? But no, Rajaram had just sat down to eat, he might as well find out what the matter was. Then Latu had second thoughts; what if Rajaram became furious for not being told at once? What should he do?

With Shashi absolutely terrified, Latu decided Rajaram simply had to be informed. They proceeded towards his room, running up the stairs.

Rajaram had just splashed some water on his face, washed his hands, and sat down to eat. Following the required rituals, he sprinkled drops of water on the ground around his plate and began to crumble the perfect disc of rice on it. Slender, white grains. Two bowls next to the plate had a potato and cauliflower preparation and curried rohu fish, respectively.

Then suddenly, a pounding on the door. And Latu's voice….

'Shaheb…. Shaheb….'

Rajaram was irked. Latu had brought him his dinner only a few minutes ago. What could possibly have happened to make him rush back? His voice indicated he had rushed here. Still sitting where he was, Rajaram asked, 'What is it? I was about to eat.'

'Didi isn't opening the door,' came the reply.

As soon as he heard this Rajaram dipped his fingertips in the drops of water he had just sprinkled on the floor and shot to his feet to open the door.

'My goodness! Why not?'

Shashi was standing next to Latu. Fear was writ large on both their faces. Even on this pre-winter night, they were sweating.

'Took her…her food, banged on the door, she didn't open it,' said Shashi. 'Called her loudly, not a sound. Looked like the lamps weren't lit either.'

The fear felt by the servant and maid infiltrated Rajaram's body like a contagion. He was unable to determine what he should do. He was frightened instantly, his hands beginning to tremble. His legs too. This was how he usually reacted to the smallest of fears. Annoyance mingled with dread in him. Rajaram wondered whether Latu and Shashi could tell that he was afraid.

'Let's find out,' said Rajaram and led the way to Krishnabhabini's room.

When they arrived outside, Rajaram looked around and began to call her by her name. At first it was just him, then Shashi and Latu joined in. This went on for some time. Then Rajaram put his hand on the door and called her name gently. He tried to lift the slats on the window and open it, succeeding in his attempt. But with no light inside, nothing could be seen through the dark purple glass at this hour of the night. Taking the lamp from Shashi, Rajaram peered through the bars and the window pane. He did this at both the windows. No result.

Left with no choice, Rajaram and Latu began pushing at the door with the intention of breaking it. But the defense erected on the other side appeared particularly strong. Not all the strength they applied in this manner worked. The door shook, fit to burst open any moment—but it did not. Finally, Rajaram gave an instruction. 'Run along, Latu, and get the sickle.'

Latu fetched the sickle from the tiny room on the roof. A large knife caught his eye as he was leaving the room, so he picked it up too.

Under a collective assault from all of these, the door broke eventually.

Entry.

And then nothing but stupefaction.

In the beam thrown by the lamp in Shashi's hand, the sight of Krishnabhabini hanging from the joist overhead became clear slowly. There used to be a small chandelier hanging from the ceiling, it was on the floor now. And Krishnabhabini's body was hanging from the hook of the chandelier.

'Bini wouldn't have been able to reach the hook if the bed hadn't been so high,' Rajaram muttered futilely and almost unknowingly, his voice dying.

> This, then is the fate of this body. Unbearable! It's unbearable! This too I have to witness. This incident, too, has to take place in this house. What now? What next?

They lowered Krishnabhabini's body to the bed. Rajaram seemed to feel a trace of warmth in the body. Latu's and

Shashi's expressions suggested the same. But Rajaram stopped himself, suddenly turning cautious as it occurred to him that some very important tasks had to be performed before the doctor was sent for.

'Get the rope out of here, Latu. Drop it in the river. Be careful no one sees.'

Latu removed the rope at once. Wrapping it in a length of cloth, he deposited it beneath the safe. Shashi immediately bent down and pushed it further in. By then, all of them had signed an unwritten pact of secrecy.

As soon as the rope was gone, Rajaram said in a tired-of-talking-to-someone-who-refused-to-listen tone, 'Fetch the doctor quickly. Go, Latu.'

Just as Latu was about to leave, Rajaram said, 'No, stop. Put the chandelier back where it was. And listen, don't tell anyone just yet. Even the doctor; just tell him she was ill, she suddenly got worse today. All right?'

Latu nodded and left.

At the sight of an inert Krishnabhabini in bedraggled garments, with her face pallid and her hair in disarray, Rajaram's moist eyes conjured up an image of a clay goddess being taken to the river for immersion. Drawing the teapoy placed next to the bed, Rajaram sat down on it. A cold sweat running down the body, a faint voice proclaiming: 'He severed the heads of Ravan, not one but ten….'

Rajaram was sitting in front of the corpse. Shashi stood behind him, weeping, although it was clear from her behaviour that she was only trying to cry. In truth, she was frightened, terribly frightened. She had never experienced such fear before. For now, she would be relieved if she could run away. She wanted to keep her responsibility to her employer at a distance.

But no, there was no escape.

As soon as he entered, Kedarnath, the doctor, appeared certain of the touch of death in the body. Shashi had already covered it all the way to the neck, so that the congealed red mark left by the rope could not be seen. Having realized that his presence was futile, Kedarnath sat there seemingly inspecting Krishnabhabini's body only as a formality. His relationship with this family was a long one. He had seen Krishnabhabini before, although he had never really spoken to her. Although being a doctor, Kedarnath accepted death much more naturally than ordinary people, he still took all deaths personally. Instead of treating death as simply a cessation of life, every instance of it assailed him as a source of grief. As a result, somewhere within himself, he suffered deeply. Even a short while ago there was life in this body, his heart told him, and now its essence was gone. What sport was this! When it came to such thoughts, his heart made no exception for Krishnabhabini.

He checked the prone Krishnabhabini's pulse and examined her eyes by drawing the lower lids down. In between, although Rajaram or Latu did not notice this, he pressed down once or twice on the neck on either side of the chin. As he was about to touch the sheet covering Krishnabhabini, a terrified Shashi deterred him quickly with gestures signalling feminine privacy.

Kedarnath stayed for half an hour before declaring Krishnabhabini dead and proceeded to leave. When Rajaram made to offer him his fees, he refused, saying he would not accept any fees today.

'But we called you for a visit so late in the night...' said Rajaram.

'Doesn't matter; you'd better take care of things here, Rajaram. Send for me again if you need me.' Touching

Rajaram's arm fleetingly, he left. Latu escorted him back home. It was not a long way, Kedarnath lived two houses away after a right turn at the head of the street.

Latu returned to find the air of dread persisting in the room. Rajaram sat still on the teapoy, lost in thought. Shashi stood next to him. Her crying had become intermittent now, and the fear had dissipated from her expression to some extent. Latu could not tell how he should actually express his grief or whether there was any need to at all. He was still engaged in tasks—that was his duty.

A little later, without the slightest concern for whether anyone was paying attention, without even looking over his shoulder to check whether Shashi and Latu were still standing behind him, Rajaram said as though he were offering advice, 'Arrange for the cremation, it will be done tonight. Take as much money as you need from the office.'

Rajaram used to keep the money needed for monthly expenses in a safe in the office where he went over documents pertaining to his estate. His trusted servant Latu used to take money from the safe as required. The number of domestic staff had begun shrinking after the death of Rajaram's father. Although this was ostensibly on the grounds of there being no need for so many people, it was actually to reduce costs. How many people could it need to look after one person and a minor estate?

Rajaram trusted Latu deeply. He used to consider Latu capable of performing whatever tasks were needed single-handedly. So Latu remained in employment.

'All right, Shaheb. Then don't sit here sadly anymore, please eat.' Latu nudged Shashi with his arm to say the same thing to Rajaram.

'Yes, Shaheb...' Shashi began.

Cutting her off, Rajaram said, without turning to look at them, 'Don't go on and on, do as I ask you to. Go away now.'

Rajaram's instruction held more than a little annoyance. And with it, an unarticulated plea to be left alone.

Latu and Shashi left. And until they returned after having made all the arrangements, Rajaram sat like a rock next to Krishnabhabini's dead body.

The light in the room had taken on the shade of molten gold. The corpse seemed to be adorned in jewellery made of this light. Krishnabhabini was radiant now before being reduced to ashes. Rajaram felt a lump in his throat at the thought. Distractedly, and as though his speech were impeded, he began to speak: 'Didn't I tell you Bini, get rid of it. I'd made the arrangements. You didn't even wait for the kobiraj. Why did you have to do this Bini.... You've given me a shock, Bini, a big shock.... Hah!'

There were no tears in Rajaram's eyes. Suddenly, he appeared eager to blame the dead woman for her death. He let the sentences escape his lips as quickly as possible like he had a long narrative of self-defence to be articulated in a limited time. He seemed pincered by a barrage of accusations from an unknown source, holding him responsible for Krishnabhabini's death. Rajaram was already thinking of himself as the primary accused person in this incident. And it was on those terms that he was actively engaged in refuting the allegations.

An unusual situation—a silent, invisible, plaintiff and a garrulous defendant. An agitation conducted by the living, asking to be relieved of responsibility for a death. But with no judge. The judge was absent.

Absent because a judge was perhaps superfluous.

How could this come to be, how could it…. I never wanted this. I never thought this would come to pass. I want to remain composed. How shall I manage this crisis? How did all of this take place? Am I responsible? Was it because of me that she chose suicide? She never uttered a word. It never seemed that she considered me responsible. What was it then….

Rajaram's body was ice-cold. The sweat kept flowing. He could feel an ache manifesting itself in the back of his head. He shuddered from time to time. Rajaram rose from the teapoy.

∽

This was how time eroded. Eight years had passed in the blink of an eye. After his aunt, Bimala's, death eight years ago, the responsibility of looking after Krishnabhabini, who used to be dependent on her, was thrust upon Rajaram. By then he had been left utterly bereft. His father had died several years ago, and he had never even set eyes on his mother, for Dyaneshwari Debi had died immediately after giving birth to Rajaram. Despite requests from many people who had positively entreated him, Debram had not married a second time. Nor had he displayed any interest in the company of women. He would in fact avoid the subject of women, feeling awkward, and would be on the verge of escaping whenever it came up.

Bimala had been something of a second guardian for Rajaram, filling in for his absent mother. Debram used to be taciturn, grave, and imposing. Any command of his was impossible for Rajaram to ignore, it was imperative to follow it. It was in these circumstances that Bimala had grown into a substitute for Rajaram's mother. It was not as though he had ever bared his heart to anyone, but with Bimala he appeared to let his guard down. His very existence seemed simpler. All his suppressed thoughts could be disclosed to her at any time—this was what Rajaram always felt intensely in his aunt's company. Although the feeling of I-can-say-it-whenever-I-want was in itself sufficient, Rajaram had stopped there. He had never actually told Bimala what lay in his heart.

Bimalasundari was an authentic beauty. Even though she was no longer young when Rajaram saw her for the first time, he could appreciate her loveliness. There were signs of wrinkles on her fair skin, her hair had begun to turn silver, her gait faltered. But she remained a refined beauty. In the afternoon, she would let down her long hair, sit in a corner of the veranda, and slice betel nuts with a nutcracker while chewing on a paan. As she sliced the betel nut she would pop the pieces into her mouth. The sounds of her chewing and the nuts being sliced, the fragrance of the paan, and the cylindrical shape assumed by the sunbeams filtering through the lattice work in the veranda would entrance a young Rajaram. Everything seemed connected, it was not possible to consider anything in isolation. All of these phenomena seemed to materialize, one after the other, one within the other, in an unending line. Bimala's chewing on the paan and the sunlight—identical. And with these two, his presence and existence at that time—also identical. The collective images from that time, the recollections of every single day, were untarnished in Rajaram's memory. It was as though he could recount each of those days individually.

Sometimes he wondered strongly—memory can grow weaker with age, could it not? In that case, when someone had reached the end of their life, how many of the days they had left behind would remain alive in their memory? How many could remain? He himself could still remember most of the days he had lived through.

No one can discover each and everything about the members of their family at once. Such information comes to be revealed slowly. Through other people, other channels. That is when a long-held impression about a person changes gradually. One may feel extreme rage and aversion for someone while lavishing love and sympathy on someone else. Thus, it was that, as he grew older, Rajaram learnt some things about Bimala's life that made him sorry for her. Bimala had told him herself.

Rajaram's grandfather had disowned his eldest son, Sitaram, because of his licentious and profligate lifestyle. Leaving home in anger and resentment at this loss of honour, he went away to Jessore. The incident took place seven or eight years after Sitaram's marriage. At Jessore, he began to work as a secretary to a British mercantile officer. He bought some land and even married a second time. Barring the little information that trickled down occasionally, nothing more was known about his life.

One day, about two years before Rajaram's father's death, news came of Sitaram's demise. The cause or manner of his death was unknown. Debram made no effort to communicate with his elder brother's 'unknown' widow. He was thoroughly disgusted with Sitaram.

Although Bimala had been abandoned by her husband, it was with his family that she had found sanctuary. Sitaram had spurned her, but everyone else accorded her great respect. Bimala had come into this house for the first time at the age of twelve. She had seen a good deal and tolerated a great many things too, but never neglected her duties. However, she had never tried to establish her authority. Bimala had first met Debram when he was an adolescent boy, which was why she used to love him like a son. On his part, Debram was always attentive to his sister-in-law's needs and looked after her with great care.

Bimala had no children, she was sterile. She had to stomach many harsh words from Sitaram because of this. He left her without a thought about her well-being, and they never met again. Whenever Debram received any news of him, he let Bimala know with his eyes fixed on the ground, as though he was responsible for what had happened. Despite everything, Bimala remained serene and unperturbed, never complaining or expressing her resentment. Perhaps she had become so detached mentally, so distanced from the conventional expression of feelings, that not even the news of her husband's death could make her lose her composure. All she did was to go to the river, remove all traces of being a married woman, and don the attire of a widow. Not a single tear was to be seen in her eyes as she performed these acts.

One day, a new member joined Rajaram's family. Her name was Krishnabhabini. She had not come of her own accord; she was brought here. When Bimala introduced Krishnabhabini, who had just come of age, to the residents, a young Rajaram asked no investigative questions. His father must have known more, yet he did not ask his father either. His childless aunt must have adopted the girl, Rajaram concluded. Krishnabhabini's oval eyes, waist-length hair, coppery complexion, and physical appearance would have caught anyone's eye, and Rajaram was no exception. But he seemed to consciously evade such matters or thoughts. A strange situation, comprising a mixture of some embarrassment and some annoyance. That a woman he did not know had started living in the same house was most discomfiting to Rajaram. An unseen, unarticulated restriction seemed to have been imposed on his movements. Someone appeared to be keeping him under surveillance, or perhaps it was he who was keeping someone under surveillance. Utterly uncomfortable.

Rajaram's first meeting with Krishnabhabini, a few days after her arrival, was a strange one. One afternoon, Latu informed Rajaram that his aunt had sent for him. As soon as he entered, he saw Krishnabhabini standing by the bed with her head lowered. Her hair wasn't tied up. It covered her breasts.

Smiling gently at Rajaram, Bimala said, 'You must have seen her here by now, Raja.'

'Yes, I have. But we have not been introduced.'

'I know; that's why I asked you here. This is my spiritual daughter, Krishnabhabini.'

'Spiritual daughter?'

'That's right, spiritual daughter.' With a pleasant smile, she added, 'At last you have a sister.'

That was the first time Rajaram met a woman not from the family, his first such acquaintance. He didn't say a word to her that day. Or perhaps he could not. He had merely managed to glance at Krishnabhabini and curve his lips slightly in an effort to smile.

Since then, Rajaram had been seeing this girl, some fifteen years younger than him, every day. Twenty years had passed after that, but they had never conversed much. Whatever few exchanges there had been in the beginning had dwindled for obvious reasons as both of them grew older.

Whenever he ran into Krishnabhabini, Rajaram never knew what to tell her or how to say it. He could only continue with a conversation that had been repeated many times: 'Any news, Krishnabhabini?'; 'Are you well?'; and so on.

One day, Krishnabhabini said to him unexpectedly, 'Why do you call me by this mouthful of a name? Don't you find it difficult?'

Rajaram smiled. 'What should I call you then? Do you have a nickname?'

'No, but your aunt used to call me Bini.'

'Excellent, I shall also call you by that name from now on.'

But not having anything suitable to tell Krishnabhabini, Rajaram used to avoid her as much as he could. This imposed distance had turned them increasingly into strangers. Sometimes Krishnabhabini would appear in the veranda, freshly bathed, with her hair wet. If Rajaram happened to run into her at this time, he would leave as swiftly as possible, all but hiding himself.

On a sunless afternoon towards the end of spring, Rajaram stood alone in the veranda. The clouds had configured themselves in the sky. Rain was imminent. It turned dark, with distinct signs of a northwester. But it was still very hot and sultry, with no breeze. The leaves hung immovably from the trees. The birds returned home, chirping incessantly.

Suddenly Rajaram heard Krishnabhabini's voice. In song: *'Raghava may not take you in / But you are never helpless / Look deep within your heart / Raghava lives in there.'*

Rajaram loved the tappa, he was very fond of Ramnidhi Gupta's songs. He had heard tappa songs composed by others too and was familiar with almost all of the recent songs from various sources. But this song was unknown. He could not identify the composer. Rajaram knew that Krishnabhabini sang, he had heard her sing earlier too. But today he listened closely for the first time. It was as though she was singing specifically for his benefit.

Rajaram walked on towards Krishnabhabini's room. It was quite dark now, the large pillar in the veranda throwing a big shadow. All the shadows merged, as though someone had sprinkled ink over everything.

The door was ajar, the windows closed. Krishnabhabini sat on a carpet on the floor. The song poured out of her throat unrestrained, a pure emotion. '...*If the thread of love is strong / Do not fear not seeing him / A glimpse is but the body / What matters is the heart....*'

Rajaram stood still in the doorway, his eyes on Krishnabhabini. The lamps in the room had not been lit yet, and Rajaram's shadow plunged it further into darkness. Krishnabhabini was unmoved. Her physical form was visible even in the dark. A wave kept surfacing from her body, only to ebb again.

The notes rose, the notes fell. Rajaram listened in silence, not daring to move even slightly lest he interrupt the music. The song drew to a close. And Krishnabhabini remained sitting. Silent. The end of her sari had dropped slightly from her shoulder. Even in the darkness her neck and the upper swell of her breasts were clearly visible. Although her complexion was dark, at that moment it suddenly seemed to Rajaram that the neck and what lay below it were the brightest parts of Bini's body. The thought thrilled and aroused him. 'He severed the heads of Ravan, not one but ten....'

Getting hold of himself the very next moment, he rapped lightly on the door.

Krishnabhabini was startled.

'Oh. Dada!'

'Did I frighten you?' Rajaram was caught unaware by Krishnabhabini's reaction. He felt he had done something wrong, that he should have announced his arrival. Instead, his secret assignation had been discovered. Rajaram attempted to make the situation normal, clearing his throat and feigning laughter, 'He he…I happened to hear you sing…so….'

Krishnabhabini had composed herself by now. She had been a little taken aback as well. Rajaram had never been here to listen to her sing, not once in all these years. 'Yes…you know, not frighten exactly, I wasn't paying attention, that's all.'

'What I came to ask Bini is who taught you this song? Who composed it?' Rajaram had been standing outside the door all this while. Now he stepped in.

'No one taught me this song.'

'What do you mean no one taught you? Who composed it then?'

'I composed it myself; I made up the tune.'

Rajaram was astonished at Krishnabhabini's answer and the readiness with which she replied.

'You composed it!'

'I did.'

'Hmm…excellent…I assumed it was someone else, it's very good.'

'I was planning to visit women in their homes, read the holy books with them, and sing for them. Shoima educated me. That was when I began composing songs.'

'Who is Shoima?'

'Your aunt.'

'I've never heard you call her by that name.'

'How much time have you spent with us, Dada? How many times have you spoken to us?'

Rajaram didn't reply.

Although Krishnabhabini had not asked for Rajaram's questions and praise, they encouraged her briefly.

'I have more songs; do you want to hear?'

A cool breeze had sprung up. Forked lines of lightning appeared in the sky as soon as Krishnabhabini uttered the word 'hear'. It was behind Rajaram's head, so he didn't see it. What he saw was the scene lit up by a purple flash.

Krishnabhabini saw both.

There was a deafening clap of thunder.

A torrential downpour began.

'Another time, Bini,' said Rajaram and left.

˷

And then it happened. Last year. It was completely unforeseen. No one was prepared for it. Like a bolt from the blue it came, the chain of events unfolding in an instant even before anyone knew what was happening. Yet it changed so many things.

It was the night before Kali Puja.

Evening had descended, and Rajaram had just woken up from his siesta. He sat quietly on his bed for some time, feeling far from cheerful. He was overcome by ennui, a sense of exhaustion. Had the sensation come over him while he was asleep or after he had woken up? Rajaram couldn't tell.

It was getting dark. Latu never brought the lamps until Rajaram asked for them. Such were the instructions to ensure Rajaram's slumber wasn't disturbed. But it wasn't just a question of interruption, he enjoyed lying in the dark. It made him feel he had separated himself from the world outside, as though he had shielded himself from it. And yet he could perceive everything—what was going on, what others were doing, whether it was morning, evening, or night. A joyous sensation.

His shawl was hanging at the head of the bed. Wrapping it around himself, Rajaram paced up and down for some time. A thought had suddenly occurred to him. Stopping, he sat down on the bed and stretched his arms and legs. Then he drank some water before opening the door and calling out, 'Latu, bring the lamps, Latu.'

He was about to retreat into his room when he thought he spotted a glow of lights in the courtyard. Who was it? What were they up to? Rajaram decided to take a look. From the veranda, he spotted Krishnabhabini arranging lamps in a circle in the middle of the courtyard. Oh, of course! It was the eve of Kali Puja, the night of Bhoot Chaturdashi. Lamps had to be lit. It was a ritual. Very well then.

Rajaram was about to return to his room, but instead, for some reason he found himself walking towards the steps leading down from the veranda. Descending to the yard, he stopped.

He found Krishnabhabini kneeling as she lit the lamps. The end of her sari kept slipping off her left shoulder. Becoming aware of Rajaram's sudden presence, she hastily adjusted her sari, offering a faint smile. But after a while, it slid shamelessly off her shoulder yet again. After trying one or two times to put it back in its place, Krishnabhabini gave up eventually and concentrated on what she was doing.

Rajaram neither smiled back nor spoke in response to Krishnabhabini's smile. He only kept his eyes fixed on her, for a silent explosion seemed to be taking place within him.

Krishnabhabini's face and neck were lit by the lamps. Her cleavage was conspicuous. Her skin was a tempting and open expanse, an invitation for unrestricted exploration. Rajaram felt his blood pounding; he was overwhelmed by an indescribable urge to which he was deeply desirous of surrendering his body. He had never experienced such a sensation before—what was this he was feeling today? He was not remotely prepared for such an experience. The situation demanded that he do something, but what? He couldn't tell. What could he possibly do now?

'He severed the heads of Ravan, not one but ten….'

Unknown to himself, his hand stole to the spot.

A thought asserted itself unbidden to his mind—no sooner did it occur to him that Krishnabhabini was his 'sister' than he realized it was an imposed relationship. They shared neither parents nor a bloodline. But…but why these thoughts at this moment?

Rajaram found no satisfactory answers. He could think of just the one solution. Only a conversation with Krishnabhabini right now could abate this agitation. He was personally rather startled and embarrassed at the intense expression of an unprecedented desire, an unarticulated passion.

'I want to hear you sing today, Bini. It's the night of Bhoot Chaturdashi, a real carnival.'

'What's that? What on earth is a canival?'

'Oho, not canival, but carnival. An immeasurable ecstasy, a magnificent celebration.'

Krishnabhabini could make no sense of what Rajaram was saying. In any case, she found him something of an eccentric. Having lived in the same residence as him for many years, she had long witnessed signs of curious behaviour in him. Who knew what came over him ever so often? He began to recite lines from Kashidas. Sometimes he paced up and down madly in the veranda and even in the courtyard. Now and then, he left the house without informing anyone. At other times he locked himself in his room for hours on end, and no one had the power to persuade him to come out unless he wanted to. He had an unpredictable temper too—sometimes all was well, but when he became furious, no one dared to face him for four or five days. And now he had begun uttering this new word: carnival.

'All right, when should I sing for you?'

'At night…after dinner. Will it be inconvenient?'

'No, why should it be inconvenient? It's not as though I fall asleep as soon as I go to bed. And I don't go to bed right after dinner. Come to my room.'

'No, I shall not go. You will come to my room. That's where I'll hear you sing.'

Lighting the fourteenth and last lamp and gazing at its flame, Krishnabhabini nodded slightly. 'Very well.'

'When the stars come out at night / my heart dances in delight / come into my arms then / feel no fear or shame….'

'Who gave you this bracelet?'

Rajaram threw the question at Krishnabhabini even though she was singing. The hour was well past midnight and inching towards dawn. It was Krishnabhabini's third song of the night.

Shortly after dinner, she had appeared in Rajaram's room as promised. They were together like this for the first time, in the same room, at night. On opening the door, Rajaram had gazed at Krishnabhabini for a while. Sometimes some wishes were realized—even though they remained until the moment of realization—nothing but wishes. Wishes that were not even pursued, but were no less living for that reason. Constantly alive, in fact.

Although Krishnabhabini was annoyed, she kept it from her expression and paused her singing to answer in a low voice, 'Shoima.'

Like a bolt from the blue, an unprovoked rage sprang up within Rajaram. It came without warning. He could never fathom the reason for his temper and found no reasonable cause for it tonight, but he suddenly had the urge to attack Krishnabhabini with words. He would find pleasure in such an assault. And so, he did.

'Who are you hoarding all your beauty for Bini?'

The question as unexpected as this display of anger. Krishnabhabini was bewildered and hurt to an even greater degree.

'What manner of question is this that you ask, Dada?'

'I don't know about manner...just answer me.'

'Are you saying this because you just saw this piece of jewellery? But I've been wearing it for a long time...it's just that you don't notice.'

'It's not that.'

'What is it then? You've never talked to me this way before, never asked such a question.'

'Just because I haven't so far there's no logical reason to assume I never will.'

'I'm not talking of logic.'

'What are you talking about then?'

'Never mind.'

'Answer me. What is it then?'

'I'm not hoarding any beauty for anyone.'

Krishnabhabini looked forlorn, there was melancholy in her heart.

'Show me the bracelet...take it off...did Narayan make it?'

'Yes,' said Krishnabhabini, handing Rajaram the ornament.

He turned it over in his hand and examined it. And that was when it began—the fragrance of Krishnabhabini's body, crushed into metal, infiltrated Rajaram's senses. Mingling with the air, it played near his nostrils. He felt himself growing hotter. The scent of Krishnabhabini's perspiration and of her skin was making him lose all his restraint. His nether parts were throbbing under the onslaught of arousal. He could not take it anymore.

Laying the ornament down on the pillow, an aggressive Rajaram abruptly pushed Krishnabhabini, who was sitting in front of him, down on the bed. It happened so swiftly that before Krishnabhabini knew what was going on—in her distraction she had not even been looking at Rajaram—he had planted his body on hers with alacrity.

'Oh...what are you doing, Dada?'

'As if you never wanted it.' Rajaram's voice was unconcerned, he spoke bluntly.

When an undeniable truth kept unacknowledged by choice is suddenly uttered, as though freed from its fetters, it stops us in our tracks. All movements cease. A truth such as this can rob us of speech for a moment, it can stifle the flow of words. Krishnabhabini's complete silence and lack of response after Rajaram's rebuke was an illustration of this.

> He severed the heads of Ravan, not one but ten.
> But with the creator's boon they sprouted again....

'Carnival! I can't be anything but the carnival!'

The day the first signs of pregnancy appeared, Krishnabhabini went directly to Rajaram's room without any preamble. Her eyes held an unspoken message. The day had progressed several hours by then.

Without wasting much time wondering how to inform Rajaram, Krishnabhabini told him directly. His expression as she talked to him offered no way of knowing whether he was listening or not. His gaze was blank.

When she was done, Rajaram told her firmly, 'Get rid of it Bini, I'll make all the arrangements.' He spoke in a way that suggested he needn't have listened to Krishnabhabini talk for such a long time, that his reply was predetermined.

Krishnabhabini was silent. She had not expected such a dry and harsh response.

'Did you hear what I said?'

Krishnabhabini nodded slightly. With a single glance at Rajaram, she was made to leave the room. She had nothing more to say.

She had taken only a single step when there was a knock on the door. 'Shaheb…Shaheb!'

It was Latu, holding a tiny kitten. Milk white, with two black patches near its head.

'Found this one outside the gate, Shaheb…I don't know who left it there. Couldn't just leave it on the road, so I brought it to you.'

Rajaram was silent. Then he gestured for the kitten to be given to him.

He proceeded to examine the kitten, as though its arrival

was scheduled, and he was only comparing the features of the creature in his lap with the information already in his possession.

The kitten looked around with its tiny eyes, waving its legs, meowing.

'Of course, why should you leave it there? I'm keeping it,' Rajaram spoke finally.

Krishnabhabini glanced at Rajaram once more during this exchange, even though he was now absorbed in the kitten in his lap.

She left for her room.

Walking about with the kitten for a while, Rajaram addressed it. 'I've given you a name. Simantini.'

Latu was still standing there.

'Understood?' Rajaram told him. 'Her name is Simantini. She will live with us from now on.'

'Understood, Shaheb. Shimuntini.'

༄

Rajaram had informed Raash, the kobiraj, about the need to perform an abortion for Krishnabhabini. He had to maintain utmost secrecy. The kobiraj, who lived across the Hooghly, was a family connection who had treated Rajaram's grandfather and father too. Rumour was that he had long gone past a hundred years in age. He was both a doctor and a tantra practitioner.

At first Rajaram had thought of going himself, but then he realized he would never be able to tell Raash what had happened. Partly out of respect, partly out of fear and embarrassment. Finally, he sent word through Latu, putting down the truth and mentioning the purpose in a letter. Latu was illiterate, and hence a suitable choice for this task.

Latu and Shashi were told Krishnabhabini was ill.

In any event, the kobiraj had promised to visit, sending brief instructions on the reverse side of Rajaram's letter. The primary requirement was a big room and a large pot in which a huge quantity of onions could be boiled. Krishnabhabini would have to sit on a pile of boiling onions.

Rajaram had made arrangements complying with all the instructions.

But Krishnabhabini hanged herself three days before the kobiraj was due to visit.

⁑

The door opened at the lightest touch. Inside, Latu saw Rajaram standing in front of Krishnabhabini's body. The teapoy was behind him. Rajaram seemed to be tottering, as though he would fall any moment unless someone supported him. Was Latu's employer mumbling something? Latu couldn't decipher it, but Rajaram appeared to be muttering to himself. He had not even registered Latu's entrance. When Latu realized Rajaram had not noticed him, he decided to go back outside the room and knock on the door. He tiptoed out accordingly.

Rapping on the door, Latu said, 'All the arrangements have been made, Shaheb.'

Rajaram turned, his legs still unsteady, his eyes dull. He had heard Latu. He walked out of the room slowly, casting a glance over his shoulder at the door. Then he left.

'Make the preparations,' he said, 'I'll be back.' His voice was sombre.

One person can often be the cause of the death of another, but sometimes it can also be the case that death needs someone to usher it in. Or that a person needs death. And another person can be the medium between these two entities. Perhaps Rajaram was the medium—the medium of death. This was the notion tumbling about in his head during Krishnabhabini's journey to the crematorium. It was not the custom, but he accompanied her. He did not perform the last rites himself, getting the man who disposed of dead bodies to do it. In any case, Rajaram's family was not related by blood to Krishnabhabini, so there was no question of following the after-death rituals.

When he got home that night, Rajaram bathed and went to bed in a hurry. Before his bath, he sprinkled some water from the Ganges on himself, which he had earlier collected in a pitcher. He sprinkled a few drops on his bed too before lying down on it. His eyes alighted on Simantini crouching in a corner. She had followed Rajaram briefly while he was walking in front of Krishnabhabini's body bedecked with flowers. Spotting her, Rajaram had scooped the kitten up in his arms and passed her to Latu to be deposited back in the room. Simantini had not emerged since then, lying curled in the corner. She sat up now on spotting Rajaram. The cat looked petrified—she seemed to have witnessed or comprehended death, even if it was a human's, for the first time in her life.

Rajaram lifted her to his bed, stroking her head gently.

'There's going to be a carnival, Simantini, a carnival,' muttered Rajaram as he dropped off to sleep.

The sky was grey. The day was knocking on the doors of dusk, but it wasn't clear what time it was. Three gigantic kites flew in the air, tossing and tumbling wildly. The sky turned from grey to black, dark clouds were amassed together, swollen in form, all of them. Frequent bursts of lightning. A purple hue in the sky. Warm surroundings.

Suddenly the sound of drum beats became audible—exactly the kind you could hear when Durga was worshipped. Who was playing the drum? Where? What was the occasion? And now what was this…the sound of conch shells too? Rajaram tried to listen closely. Where was all this going on? Possibly from downstairs. How could something like this be taking place in his own house without his knowing anything about it? What could they be celebrating?

Rajaram tried to look over the balustrade of the veranda but could see nothing. He climbed down the stairs, the sounds becoming louder. Soon it became obvious that the number of people playing drums was not half a dozen or even a hundred, but over a thousand. They were beating their drums together on the thakurdalan where the deities were worshipped. Rajaram was overwhelmed by the sight. Countless women, young and middle-aged, all around him, were blowing into conch shells. They seemed to be in a trance, oblivious to his presence and completely immersed in their activities. There was a layer of white paint on their faces. They were dressed in white saris with red borders, with vermilion in the parting of their hair. Ornaments of gold adorned their arms and necks, and their soles were outlined in red dye.

The drummers' faces were whitened too. The corners of their eyes had been elongated by lines of paint stretching to their ears. Silky white bird feathers fluttered like flags from the ends of their drums. They were playing like madmen.

Latu and Shashi were nowhere to be seen.

Suddenly, as though a dam had been breached, Rajaram saw blood-red water gushing out from one corner of the courtyard. In moments the courtyard was filled with red water, blood water.

The women who had gathered had begun ululating. In response to them, the drummers speeded up their rhythm. They began dancing—first one, followed by a few others, then many more, and finally all of them.

It began to pour with rain. The raindrops fell loudly into the pool of red. Rajaram could hear water colliding with water.

Suddenly he observed a woman, completely naked, about to jump from the roof. Who was she? The answer was evident instantly—it was Krishnabhabini. In a moment, she had leapt into the red water and vanished under it. Rajaram was about to reach out and scream, but at that moment, he discovered he had become completely paralysed, too fatigued to move. Not a word or even a sound escaped his lips. His body was numb.

The ululation, conch shells, drum beats, and the hammering of the rain rose to a crescendo. And the thunder asserted itself in the sky.

THREE

A pale glow made its presence felt slowly across a sky shrouded in darkness. One or two birds had begun chirping. The air was still cool and fragrant with ittar. The room had filled with a trace of soft moisture. There was no lamp on the stand, and Rajaram had no desire to light one either. Despite the predominance of darkness, the partial existence of a dim source of illumination was evident. Visibility was not completely absent. Simantini had woken up. Sitting on her hind legs, she licked her front paws. Turning on his side, Rajaram sat up and watched Simantini with the eye of an observer.

Very slowly, with great patience, she licked each of her claws clean. Once the forepaws were done, she flopped down on her side and began licking the hind paws. Rajaram had seen her do this many a time. Still, he felt a new sense of wonder today at the sight of Simantini's concentrated licking of her own feet.

> Do they ruminate at this time? The white of her body has turned to silver in the near darkness. It is flashing. Now and then when she turns this way her glittering green eyes signal that it is time.

The carnival!

'Come, Simantini...come to me,' said Rajaram

At once she came up to his bed. Bending a little, Rajaram picked her up in his arms. Simantini's body was as soft as cotton wool, her fur was as smooth as silk.

Simantini meowed softly now and then. Holding her plump cheek against his own, Rajaram said, 'The appointed hour is almost here. You have to remain here. You have to be awake. You have to witness everything. You are my heir.'

Rajaram paused.

Then, invigorated by the notion that his cat was eagerly participating in the conversation, Rajaram said, 'Your children are my heirs too. I've considered them as well. Give birth to them here…don't let them be fetched from other places. I won't be here after all, and there's no one else to do it either.'

Simantini had lain down on the bed with her head between her forelegs. She was gazing obliquely at the window, occasionally lifting a paw to brush away something from near her nose.

'Won't you miss me when I'm gone? You'll never see me again.' At this question Simantini turned to look at Rajaram, or so he thought. Without waiting for a response, he stroked her head lightly, grazing it with one finger from the ears to the region above her eyes. The two black patches had created a clear section on Simantini's head, like a parting in the hair. Rajaram ran his finger up and down the white line between them.

A little later he wrapped a shawl around himself and left his bed. Freed of the weight, the pillow Rajaram had been leaning against shifted slightly, startling Simantini. But the very next moment she realized what it was and went back to her position on the bed.

Rajaram went up to the window and opened one of the panes fully. Daylight was imminent, a blue glow had spread across the sky. It had never occurred to him before that the advent of dawn was a process. He had never been able to wake up at this hour; he could count the number of 'dawns' he had seen on the fingers of one hand. Today was one of those rare days when Rajaram was gazing at dawn. The illustrated and annotated carnival would be revealed to him slowly now. Preparations were underway, the stage was being set, and the actors were getting dressed.

Setting the window pane back to its earlier position and drawing his shawl tightly around himself, Rajaram turned to his right and immediately saw the drafts of the letter piled next to the mahogany table. All composed many years ago, addressed to Dwarkanath Tagore. They already seemed to have taken on the appearance of ancient birch. Thick layers of dust had accumulated on them, changing the colour of the paper. The room had not been cleaned in years, and Rajaram had not even glanced at the letters in all this time.

A gust of wind collided with the window panes, flinging them wide open.

Startled once again, Rajaram felt as though he were spilling out of his body. In a flash, he turned to look at the window. Its swift opening made him feel embarrassed, as though someone had seen him naked, as though he had disrobed in public without warning.

Simantini had also jumped up at the sound. She stared at the window in surprise.

> Their sense organs are sharper than ours. Has Simantini sensed something?

There was no way of knowing. After a glance, Simantini stretched out on the bed again.

The gust of wind did not last long. Rajaram wrapped his shawl around himself even more closely, as though he was protecting his modesty from invisible but probing eyes. Then drawing the window panes back to their previous position, he advanced slowly towards the pile of drafts. A small tower of sheets of paper tied with a red ribbon.

Rajaram loosened the knot. Dust flew into the air, invading his nostrils, along with its smell. The sheets crackled. They smelt of old paper, of ink. Rajaram brought them to his nose and inhaled. The dust went in, tickling the nasal passage. Then he lay them flat on the table. Ah! A different world altogether.

> Rajaram, Rajaram, this is a different world, a different universe. You entered but didn't go in. Was it because you could not? You only touched the surface. No, not even touched. In your imagination, you went close, but you didn't go farther. Was it because you could not? Why not, Rajaram? This was the world you desired, after all. If you could have gone into it your identity, your very existence, would have changed slowly. Just as you had wanted them to. There were so many possibilities, so much hope, Rajaram. But it didn't materialize. None of it materialized.

Prince Dwarkanath Tagore. A descendant of Nilmani Tagore. Dwarkanath of Jorasanko. Son of Rammani Tagore. Adopted son of the once great babu, Ramlochan Tagore.

Every one of the letters began with an identical form of address: 'To Babu Dwarkanath Tagore, Esquire'.

Rajaram was worked up now....

He severed the heads of Ravan, not one but ten.
But with the creator's boon they sprouted again.

Had Dwarkanath Tagore seen the carnival?

FOUR

There was a song you heard often back then, circulating like other popular songs. Many said it had been composed by Rupchand Pakshi, that he alone was capable of it. Some in fact had no doubt about it, they were certain it was Rupchand's. People listened to various kinds of songs at the time—the panchali, the half-akhrai, the dhop, and the compositions of kobials. Rajaram had heard many of them, struck by the narrative in some, the satire in others, the melody in a few. But he had not the slightest interest in learning about the composer or the source (if he didn't know it already). And so, at the preliminary stage, his customary perspective on this song saw no change. But it had become attractive to him in another way, for it had made him uncommonly curious about the most controversial person in the city then, Babu Dwarkanath Tagore. The lyrics had transgressed the borders of sarcasm, arousing the thrill of trespassing on a forbidden world of conundrums in Rajaram's mind.

> 'What's the pleasure in that red water?
> Ask Tagore & Company.
> What do we know of the qualities of wine?
> Ask Tagore & Company.'

Red water. Although he had neither seen nor tasted it, Rajaram knew 'red water' was alcohol. The white men of the

East India Company called it rum. Rajaram did not know why it had this name, although he was very keen to find out. Was there a motive behind using a name that sounded like a Hindu god's? Had the white men done it deliberately? Rajaram did not know a single person who could give him relevant information. Eventually, he felt no urge or need to learn more. What was in a name after all? Rajaram's interest in rum had taken a different direction by then. As a drink, the red liquid had failed to attract him sufficiently. Yet he was intrigued by the process—the production, presentation, and its associated business. Especially since Dwarkanath Tagore himself was involved in the trade of 'red water'.

Rajaram had been drawn to the idea of business years ago. He had heard of businessmen, Bengali businessmen. Several of them. He was deeply interested in them and in their work. But strange as it may sound, he had not yet set eyes on any of them. He yearned to see them in person to learn in detail about their business methods. He had long harboured the desire to make these enquiries.

At first, it was alcohol that had taken Rajaram's fancy as an avenue of business. He had no reasonable answer to the question of why alcohol, but what he did have was a deep and abiding interest. Still, he had considerable doubts about whether his near and dear ones would accept a business venture in alcohol. He was just past twenty then and exceptionally enthusiastic about going into business.

Rajaram had been supervising his father's land holdings since his teenage. They were absentee landlords. By now, he was accustomed to dealing with ryots and managers. It had been awkward initially. But as time passed, the awkwardness gave way to practiced ease. Everyone beneath him in the hierarchy was in fact older than him, which made it difficult for him to decide how to talk to them. But things fell into place once he began working with them and giving them instructions. It wasn't as though he enjoyed any of this, since he was unable to shed the feeling that all this responsibility had been imposed on him. Let things go on the same way for now. But he would have to get out of here and pursue some other activity.

Debram was no tyrannical landowner. His attitude was completely unlike that of a landlord, he was a timid, God-fearing man. Even though he had no trouble collecting taxes, Rajaram had never seen his father apply force to extract unpaid dues. Debram had only a nominal number of armed guards, and they too had been inherited from his own father.

One afternoon, after they had eaten their midday meal, a memorable conversation took place between father and son. Rajaram asked Debram a peculiar question, 'Have you ever seen a businessman?'

This unexpected query evoked laughter from Debram. Moving his hookah pipe away from his lips, he said, 'Why do you ask? Are they four-legged creatures?'

'Not that, but....'

'Yes, I have. Many of them. I happen to know some of them too, though none of them can match up to Dwarkanath of Mechhuabajar. Now that is a man of prowess. Landowner, owns a bank and indigo plantations too, and then he's involved in all kinds of businesses with the Company. There's Carr, Tagore and Company, and so many more. The Company holds him in high esteem too, or they wouldn't have worked with him,' Debram paused after this breathless description. Then he continued, 'I have not seen him for myself yet, but I have heard about him from various people.'

Rajaram was examining papers related to their estate as they spoke. Debram's last utterance penetrated his consciousness more intensely than usual. It shook him. A mass of resentment had accumulated within him, and now they suddenly found a release.

'You know so much. You understand so many things. Then why do you not enter any of these fields instead of only running this estate? You did not invest in Union Bank, you did not sign the petition against the Company's decision to impose a tax on untaxed land, you did not consider indigo farming despite my urging you to.'

Debram perceived the indignation in Rajaram's tone clearly. But what answer was he to give? And how? What Rajaram had said was not untrue. But would he be able to see his father's side of things? Even if Debram tried to explain, his son would not understand, or perhaps not want to understand. So Debram did not defend himself. He was not willing to say anything or justify his choice to his son. Especially since the subject had come up before.

'Why do you not start a business enterprise?' Rajaram had asked.

Debram seemed to have been prepared for the question. He already had an inkling of Rajaram's love for commerce, and had constantly warned himself to desist from encouraging this passion.

'No, I do not belong to that category, I am a humble landowner, I do not think in such exalted terms. You have to possess a different mettle for business. And then from what I have heard, there is a great deal more to it. Complicated things.' Debram's response brimmed with annoyance.

'What do you mean by complicated things or a great deal

more? Are you referring to criticism?' Rajaram continued with his questioning.

Debram nodded. 'Yes, my boy, have you not heard the song that the riff-raff have composed about Dwarkanath? He is too important to be affected, but I cannot afford such things. I have even heard some of it is true. Apparently, his farmhouse in Belgachhia is nothing short of a whorehouse…there's talk of dancing girls from both England and India, all kinds of liquor, veritable orgies day and night.'

'Power and influence beget more power and more influence. Is it prudent in this day and age to retreat from everything in fear? Do you not agree?'

'I have no wish to argue. I am content with what there is, I see nothing to be gained from pursuing other avenues. It's easy for you to say these things, but if you were to try any of it for yourself, you would find the details most troublesome. It is best to stay within one's limitations.' Debram summoned a note of firmness to his response.

'He severed the heads of Ravan, not one but ten.'

Unable to find a suitable expression, Rajaram's fury revealed itself in the form of a drop of perspiration that arose at the centre of his forehead and flowed down the bridge of his nose to his upper lip. An undefined self-loathing, both for his father and himself, was born within him at that very moment. Were they going to sire a line of cowards? Was he carrying the seed of those who would constantly shrink away from applying their own reasoning, from wielding power, simply for the sake of safety and security? Did his father carry the same seed? There were many other timid men like them in India. They too would give birth to timid children. The country would be filled with people who refused to make progress. All of them would be afraid of their secure lives being affected adversely. This trepidation would leave them imprisoned in the condition they had been born in, entrapped in the activities they were accustomed to performing. But another group would march forward boldly without doubt or fear, without caring for canards or complications. Just as Dwarkanath Tagore was doing right now. He spoke the Bengali language too, as Rajaram and his progenitor Debram did. But what a gulf of difference there was between them and him. Here was a man of the same race, speaking the same language, who had achieved so much. And they, his father and he, were dying of fear, dying by the day. Being unique meant freeing oneself from the coils of ordinariness to emerge uninhibitedly before the world. This they were not capable of.

Given the conversation they had had already, Rajaram knew only too well he would never be able to suggest setting up an alcohol business to Debram. Although he had discussed Dwarkanath Tagore with his father several times after this, the subject of business never came up. Soon after the above mentioned incident, Debram was afflicted with cholera during his biannual visit to his estate. He died there after a short, but intense, spell of suffering. There was no opportunity for treatment. He was dead by the time Rajaram arrived.

That was the first time Rajaram performed the ritual of holding a flame to the body of someone in his family. He had not had to witness his mother's death, and he had not been present at the cremation of his aunt, Bimala's, body.

At the moment of touching his father's body with the flame—when the fire came into contact with the skin—Rajaram was overcome by a surge of affection that unmoored him. It must be the same with everyone, he reflected.

Dwarkanath had set up a man named Biswanath Laha as a small businessman. He was the distributor of the alcohol made by Dwarkanath's company. Dwarkanath also used to procure all the alcohol for personal use from the same Biswanath. Rajaram had acquired this information. Immediately after his father's death he became more interested in setting up a 'red water' business than in mourning. And he was determined that if he were to go into business, it would be in partnership with none other than Dwarkanath Tagore himself.

But what route should Rajaram take? Should he meet Biswanath Laha? Or should he go directly to the Tagore residence and meet Dwarkanath himself? What also had to be taken into account was that while he would certainly have to take one of these two paths, he was doubtful which of them he was capable of following. He recollected his conversation with his father about business and the fear of criticism. He recounted his father's warning too. 'If you were to try any of it for yourself you would find the details most troublesome.'

Rajaram had now come to realize that the path he would have to traverse was paved with hesitation and fear. Should he not proceed, then? Was his father to be proved right? That would be a terrible defeat for him. A moral surrender, a personal debacle. These moments of realization were irksome. He would develop a deep rancour for his dead father. And the more he thought about these things, the more his bitterness grew. He was tempted to shower abuse on Debram; he had the urge to destroy all his father's memories. Rajaram's first thought was, let me burn his oil painting, and then I shall throw all his garments and ornaments in the fire. Let the flames devour everything, the way they had devoured his flesh.

> Fire! Fire…o flames! Burn down this house, incinerate me. Everyone. I can no longer bear the burden of this intolerable existence. Somewhere or the other a certain class of people is being created constantly. Instead of advancing a single step towards accomplishments, they retreat a hundred steps. All they seek, directly or indirectly, is security. Perhaps this class is burgeoning now in direct opposition to men like Dwarkanath. They are prepared to be spectators from the moment of their birth. Burn them down. I fall continuously into their ranks, although my desire to escape is strong. But I cannot, o fire. Even my desire is an inert one, it refuses to go forward.

Rajaram knew he had no alternative but to meet one of the two—Biswanath or Dwarkanath. His list of acquaintances was empty. He knew the names and addresses of some of his father's associates, but he did not know how to make contact with them. He also tried to convince himself that he would be deranged to assume that they would be enthusiastic about his proposal. Perhaps it was a ruse, a form of self-justification for inevitable failure. An unidentified force was dragging him backwards. Sometimes, Rajaram reflected that his father may have experienced something similar. Perhaps he too had wanted to move forward, but an essential and suitable vehicle was missing (although he did not know its true form, Rajaram had sensed the existence of this vehicle by then). It was a lack that Rajaram felt in himself too.

The rath festival was two days away. The sky was overcast. The entire city seemed sunk in a siesta. Rajaram had also stretched out in his bed, but sleep played hide and seek with him, taking turns to approach and retreat. The valance of the fan overhead swayed in the breeze coming in through the open window, sucking out his slumber, as it were. Rajaram's punkah puller sought a few days of leave during the rains every year. This time he had not been granted leave till now, since it might not be cool every day. Only in winter did the punkah puller get a long holiday. But at this time of the year, Rajaram did tell him not to operate the fan till late in the afternoon, as he had done today. The punkah puller was probably asleep.

These thoughts eventually led Rajaram into slumber. And soon afterwards, towards a dream….

It isn't the city but a village. A mound of paddy, in front of it a small hut. A blistering sun. Two men of peculiar appearance, blood-red in complexion from head to toe, dragging a limp and weary young man by his arms towards a hut. Inside, an old woman is visible, sitting on the floor, having a meal. Probably the young man's mother. The red-skinned men say something to the young man and his mother. Their expressions make it clear they are furious with rage. Rajaram cannot hear a word of what they are saying. Suddenly everything turns black.

And then the image again…the two men perspiring profusely. Strangely, the red on their skin flows with their sweat. They turn alert upon realizing this and have a quick discussion, whose conclusion they convey to the old woman. She gets to her feet, terrified, as though she's trying to stop them. But they kick her, and she is flung to the floor. Then one of the two red men pulls out an enormous sword from his garments, while the other one slaps the young man resoundingly. The man with the sword plunges it into the young man's stomach. Blood gushes out. The old woman stares, transfixed. One of the two men dispassionately asks for the plate the old woman was eating out of. It still holds some food. The man smears the blood flowing from the young man's body on this food. Then both of them stuff the food, now streaked with blood, into the old woman's mouth. They can be seen from the back, much of the colour on their bodies has run. There's no skin either. The flesh is visible.

The small hut…the granary…the blinding sun…the village…everything turns black…then Rajaram's home once again. He's pacing about. It is late at night; the lamp has grown faint. Rajaram walks from one corner of the room to the other, naked, loudly declaiming, 'He severed the heads of Ravan, not one but ten.' Rajaram trembles to see himself this way. He can tell it's all a dream, but he's simply not able to return to reality. He is deeply uncomfortable, restless. Meanwhile, someone says, there's a letter, a letter.

Rajaram woke up. A letter! This was the word that finally snapped the dream—letter. It was late afternoon now, he could feel the breeze from the fan. The punkah puller had resumed work.

Once he was awake, Rajaram realized the grotesqueness of his dream to a much greater degree. His body was covered in sweat, but the breeze from the fan comforted him. It was a relief to wake up from the nightmare, as was the pleasant breeze in his clammy state. Rubbing his eyes and face with his hands in this state of respite, a thought struck Rajaram like a flash of lightning. A letter, a letter. Why not write a letter to Dwarkanath Tagore? It was a scintillating proposition.

'He severed the heads of Ravan, not one but ten.'

It was best to write a letter. He could reveal everything about himself to Dwarkanath. He could take his time to compose the letter, there was no need to rush. Why had he not thought of a letter all this time? It hadn't even occurred to him.

> You are an imbecile, Rajaram. What were you doing all these days? What a waste. Be that as it may, get going now. Write him a letter, a letter.

Abandoning his bed, Rajaram rose to his feet, brimming with enthusiasm. He would have to write a letter to Dwarkanath Tagore. With complete details. He would ask to be a partner, he would pay his share of the capital.

'Are you awake, Dada?' Krishnabhabini knocked on the door.

Oh, Krishnabhabini's entrance at this time was not remotely desirable. After some thought—as though he was not certain whether he had heard correctly and wanted to validate his impression—Rajaram responded in a lukewarm voice, 'Yes Bini, I'm awake, I'll open the door in a moment.'

'Is everything all right?' Even as he said this Rajaram tilted his head to steal a look at the punkah puller. Gayaram was leaning against the wall, doing his work diligently.

'What I wanted to ask is, will you please go with me to Kalighat temple tomorrow or the day after?'

Rajaram was impossibly irked by this question at that moment. This, despite the vision of the prostituted woman on the way to and from Kalighat that swam up before his eyes instantly. A blowsy sari covering a rotund body. While the temple stood directly ahead. He had seen them many times on his way back with his father.

'He severed the heads of Ravan, not one but ten.'

'What are these lines from Kashidas you mutter now and then, Dada?'

Although the words had escaped his lips softly, Rajaram was embarrassed to know Krishnabhabini had heard him. He hadn't even realized when he had uttered the words.

'Never mind, you won't understand.'

'Why should I not? There must be an explanation.'

'No. Not everything has an explanation. You cannot even begin to measure the number of things that remain unexplained.'

Krishnabhabini felt no interest in discussing this further. She had asked her question cursorily. It made no difference to her whether she got an answer or not.

'Anyway, when will you go?'

Rajaram had no desire whatsoever to go to the temple. What he had done or been forced to do in his father's lifetime by way of religious rituals was enough for him. No more. Besides, personally speaking, he could be said not to be interested in the existence of god. He had not thought of god very much, and it made no difference to him whether god existed or not. The members of Young Bengal had massacred the Hindu faith. Who cared about it in the city? What did the religion itself care? But he used to admire those youngsters—spirited, talented, and inspiring. They at least did not belong to the tribe of the fearful. Nor were they the kind to accept age-old practices just because they had been followed for a long time. Rajaram quite liked them.

'No,' said Rajaram with a sigh. 'I won't go. I'll tell Nafar, he'll have the palanquin ready for you. Do you want to go tomorrow or the day after?' Rajaram paused, and then interrupted

Krishnabhabini just as she was about to speak. 'It's the rath festival the day after, so you'd better go tomorrow.'

Asking Rajaram was superfluous. Krishnabhabini had assumed his response would be negative. It had always been like this, without exception. So, she did not coax or cajole him. What use would it have been in any case? No one had the ability to turn Rajaram's no into a yes. Krishnabhabini smiled, lowered her head, and left.

As she walked away in her red-bordered plain white sari, Krishnabhabini's figure juxtaposed itself against the dark sky. A short-lived oil painting. Rajaram gazed in her direction. Not with intent. But he had become a witness to a brief magnificence, a magnificent vision.

And then, nothing but the bars on the veranda and the black sky.

*

> 'Babu Dwarkanath Tagore
>
> Sir,
>
> I am Babu Rajaram Deb—son of late Babu Debram Deb. Long—oh for long—have I wanted to establish contact with you. But my father died and only then could I do so. I want to tell you my story first. Then I will write my need….'

One day after lunch, having pondered for long over whether to put the letter in the post, or send it through a messenger, or deliver it himself, Rajaram finally chose the third option and began a letter to Dwarkanath. In English. His hold on the language was tenuous, but although he knew this, he elected it as the medium of his letter. From what Rajaram had heard of Dwarkanath's activities, lifestyle, and behaviour, it had appeared to him that an ordinary landowner like himself could not possibly address this man, even if he was a Bengali, in any language other than English. He would try to write as best as he could. He had to demonstrate fine taste. Even if only for this reason, let the acquaintance take place in English, after which Rajaram could adopt Bengali. Not that he knew which language Dwarkanath preferred in such circumstances, or would use in case they happened to meet.

Despite this reasoning, Rajaram felt a profound unease after writing the first few sentences. His English was advanced but shaky. He had relied on his limited hold over the language to translate his statements from Bengali. The outcome was stiff and stagnant and ungrammatical to boot. Rajaram could tell as much. He also knew he was unable to express himself properly, that his words had lost their efflorescence. He had the essence, but not the language to convey it. Rajaram had no trouble with Bengali, but what he required was English. Then again, he also perceived that perhaps he was only under the impression that it was a requirement when it was not in fact one. An assumption. As though he had to demonstrate a westernized sensibility and delicacy that were impossible to achieve without speaking in English. How could Rajaram write in Bengali to a man of such stature, who rubbed shoulders with the British day in and day out, who owned flourishing business enterprises, and wielded great influence?

No, it wasn't coming out right. The Young Bengalis wrote excellent English. This problem would have been solved if only Rajaram could have been a student of Hindu College. He only lacked his father's permission—

'Why should you go to Hindu College? I do not believe it is a place for academics, and my perception is being strengthened by what I hear every day.'

'Do those who go there not belong to decent families?'

'Maybe they do. But you will not go there. There is no need.'

Oh! His late father had obstructed him in so many ways. A new loathing for Debram began to generate in his heart. He felt restless, a fuse beginning to burn within him.

> I will fail, I too will fail. This time too I will not succeed…I shall not be able to do it. What are these chains I am bound by? Who will rescue me? Who is my saviour? Where is the way out?

Rajaram stopped writing and rose from the teapoy. He had begun perspiring. He flung the length of cloth covering the upper half of his body on the bed, pulled off his dhoti, letting it drop to the floor, and loosened his undergarment with a jerk.

In a state of indescribable agitation, he paced up and down the room in the nude, declaiming, sometimes loudly, sometimes softly, 'He severed the heads of Ravan, not one but ten.'

And sometimes, 'Pull harder on the punkah, Gayaram.'

Even though Gayaram, the punkah puller, could hear Rajaram's raised voice from time to time, he could not comprehend what his master was chanting. He was frightened to hear Rajaram talking to himself. Gayaram had come to Calcutta from the Rajgir area of Bihar. His Bengali was workmanlike, which enabled him to understand the commands given to him. His speed picked up, and so did the breeze from the fan.

Although it was the rainy season, it had not rained that day. There was pale sunlight. Rajaram looked out the window, not too many people were on the street at this hour. His eye fell on the area outside the front gate of a house nearby where a pile of rubbish lay in a heap. From this distance it looked like fruit or vegetable peel, along with leftover food. A stork of the greater adjutant variety was staring at it with great concentration, as though uncertain whether to sample it. Or perhaps it was so overjoyed at the sight of so much food that it couldn't make up its mind where to begin. With its long legs it strode alternately to the left and right for a close look. After quite some time of this perambulation, the stork finally directed its long beak at the discarded food.

> This adjutant stork, does it realize what it is eating, or that what it eats is what we have discarded? Does it get its sustenance only because of what we eat or what we discard? How strange it all is. I am astonished at the delight with which they consume discarded food. Do they not find it smelly? Do they not vomit? Do they not fall ill? Extraordinary!

Rajaram turned to look around his room. His glance fell on his unfinished missive. He had a strong desire to keep writing, but he withdrew of his own volition. He stumbled when it came to the language. His discomfort grew. He fidgeted.

> What next, what? Should I write? Will I succeed? I'm failing. There is so much I want to write, so much I want to say. Will I be able to convey any of it? Anything at all?

Rajaram stood still for some time. Then he went up to the desk and held its edge before picking up the pen to continue, in English, where he had left off—

'Sir, my English is not good. I know. I am not a Hindu College boy. This is the point in truth which is also my story.'

Rajaram was standing as he wrote. He was even more mortified after writing that last sentence, slumping into a sitting position on the floor. It was patterned like a chessboard—a favourite of Rajaram's. As soon as he touched the floor the coldness of the stone hit his bare buttocks like an electric shock. Now alert, he lay down supine on the floor as though to confirm the existence of this iciness and then to feel it on his entire body. The hard, lifeless stone had no hesitation in sharing its cold touch. The back of Rajaram's head, his back, and his spine felt the coldness rising from the freezing solidity of the floor.

Rajaram stretched his arms out on both sides and then his legs the same way. He had an erection.

'He severed the heads of Ravan, not one but ten.'

Rajaram's head touched the border between black and white. His eyes were fixed on the jousts. Thin lines of tears escaped the corners of his eyes and trickled down his cheeks. They rolled past his ears too and dropped like beads on the chequered floor. The drops on the right on black squares, the drops on the left on white ones.

The fan was swaying. Evening was imminent. He simply had to write the letter. But not in English anymore. Rajaram would write in Bengali now.

A new effort to compose a letter began the next day, this time in Bengali. But not in the colloquial version, Rajaram meant to employ a refined, classical mode.

I have never written in this form. What have you accomplished, what have you accomplished, Rajaram? Nothing as yet. So now that you are about to actually do something, you are faced with so much adversity. Inevitably. Can I maintain classical grammar? What is my language? Is no language mine? All languages keep retreating from me. Why? Does everyone face this? O language, language!

'To

Srijukto Babu Dwarkanath Tagore

Sir,

'I am Sri Rajaram Deb. I have been engaged for a considerable period of time now in an endeavour to write you a letter. I had initially considered composing my missive in English, but because my knowledge of the English language is not suitably advanced, I was unable to repose sufficient faith in the effort. Accordingly, I have decided to write to you in Bengali. Perhaps it is erroneous to declare that I have decided, it would be more appropriate to state that I was compelled to make this choice. For I was presented with no other alternative. I imagine and I hope that this will result in no difficulty for you. Sir, I wish to present a proposition. It is for this purpose that I am corresponding with you. But before you peruse my proposal, it is my duty to offer you some information about myself.

'Accordingly I disclose hereby to you that I am a landlord. I have inherited my estate from my father.

> Srijukto Debram Deb was a God-fearing gentleman with laudable qualities of the mind who, despite his status as the owner of an estate, engaged himself in reading the Mahabharat every morning and evening. It is with happiness that I wish to inform you that he was an ardent admirer of yours. I have heard much about you during various conversations with my departed father and at this time I also wish to inform you with the greatest of joy that I too am not only an ardent admirer of yours but also a fervent disciple....'

Having written the phrase 'fervent disciple', Rajaram began to wonder whether he had applied it correctly. He could not think of another appellation, and this one had occurred to him naturally. How else was he to communicate the depth of his devotion? The very next moment he told himself, let me complete the letter first, I can amend it afterwards. Since there is momentum now, I might as well....

> 'But allow me to allude to this later, if I may. Sir, I have been educated at home. I had harboured the desire for an education at Hindu College, in order to learn English. But in truth my father did not grant me permission. The cause of his reluctance were the Young Bengalis and their activities. Subsequently my father informed me that you too were educated at home. I was greatly soothed to learn this. And yet the niggle persists. Manmatha Babu tutored me at home on some subjects, I owe my knowledge of English to him. Possibly his teaching was of high quality, and now that he has departed his earthly abode, I do not wish to speak ill of him. But it appears me to that the environment around

one is as important as the education one receives. I am the only child of my parents, and I grew up in solitude. I have not taken a woman in marriage—this is my choice. I have no desire for an heir. Despite my father's insistence, I did not give in on reaching the age of marriage. By way of family the only person residing in my house is an orphaned young woman, a distant relative, who was given sanctuary here. As you may conjecture, I cannot study with her. I have no friends. So I have failed to acquire a polished education because of the lack of opportunities. Contemporary education does not permit personal advancement. I am confined within the boundaries of domestic life. Had that not been the case, I would have written to you in English, a suitably practical language for my purpose. I can, however, write in the language after a fashion, although I cannot speak with speed and fluency, to compensate for which I may employ an interpreter. With your permission, I shall refer to this matter subsequently.

'Sir, although my father was a good man, I have no hesitation in stating that he was excessively apprehensive in nature. He had neither the mentality nor the initiative to constantly explore and cultivate new and unknown fields in the manner that you do at present and will continue to do. He was extremely concerned about security, which is why he lacked both the courage and the strength to attempt anything new even if he possessed the requisite desire. When the Company took the decision to impose tax on untaxed land, which you and your illustrious friends took the initiative to oppose, I had urged my father, even though I was still in my youth, to support your endeavour with his signature. Even if we did not possess any untaxed land, this would draw your attention to us. I was convinced that you would peruse the list of signatories. But he did not acquiesce, he abstained by citing the Company's troublesome laws. There was nothing more I could do. I was burdened by disappointment.

'Then there was the matter of your bank. I requested my father to deposit some of his money there, but there too he was assailed by trepidation. Apparently, it was not at all safe to entrust one's wealth to such an institution, for there was no assurance of its longevity. I attempted to persuade him to join you in indigo farming, but I failed yet again. None of my efforts bore fruit. On my part, I came to the conclusion that I would never succeed in beginning or taking part in any enterprise in association with my father. As long as he was alive, there would be no change of any kind.

'But do not be offended, sir. My respect and devotion for you is and will be undiminished.'

Rajaram stopped. Not out of tiredness from writing continuously for such a long time, but because of dissatisfaction. He felt he was not representing his father correctly in the letter, that he was becoming unduly negative in his depiction of Debram's flaws. Moreover, he was becoming far too loquacious. Dwarkanath was a busy man. Why would he deign to read such a long letter? When would he have the time? Rajaram was a stranger to him. The brevity and deftness required to present himself through the medium of the written word, Rajaram realized, were not evident in his letter.

He wrote no more that day.

To Rajaram, the situation suddenly seemed exceedingly complicated. A task that had appeared relatively simple seemed to be weighing him down now. The burden made him restless, the weight was momentarily unbearable. Rajaram had experienced similar moments and situations before too. In other contexts, with other people.

He could tell clearly now that his ability to arrive at conclusions even through his negativism gave him a certain comfort—his faculties could take him to the heart of any matter much more easily, he could grasp unnoticed patterns. Rajaram was proud of this improved acumen which had enabled him to understand why his composition of the letter had been halted and that he might never get around to writing what he actually wished to.

When there is only one thing you can depend on, when it is the sole source of your expectation, the fear of it failing you is unbearable. The more its uniqueness attracts, the more troublesome these elements seem, leading to repulsion and a growing distance. Rajaram's discomfort about what he was writing unsettled him deeply, as though the only ground he could stand on had shifted beneath his feet. He did not go back to the letter for several days.

And then one day, very late in the night, Rajaram lay sleepless in bed, tossing and turning, unable to sleep, not feeling sleepy, his eyes refusing to close. There were frequent urges to urinate. He could not comprehend how so much urine had accumulated. It was a long time since he had drunk any water, but tonight he felt a persistent need to relieve himself. At this very moment, for instance. He was thinking only of his letter.

The tension of holding back his urine fuelled his thoughts about the letter. Both his hands clutched his organ between his thighs, one of them occasionally moving up to stroke his belly. Kashidas's lines leapt to his tongue—

> 'He severed the heads of Ravan, not one but ten.
> But with the creator's boon they sprouted again.'

Finally, Rajaram rose to his feet. He simply had to let all the urine out, it was impossible to hold back any longer.

The night was silent, except for a solitary sound, like the cry of crickets. Who knew where it was coming from? Rajaram opened the door and found the punkah puller dozing. Still, he kept working the rope of the fan, mechanically and with great skill. Rajaram walked towards the toilet with a lamp. No sooner had he taken a few steps than oh! That smell… suddenly, after all this time.

This toilet was used only by Rajaram and, before his death, by Debram. The women had another lavatory to themselves. There used to be a sharp stench in Debram's urine which would persist even after buckets of water had been poured. It was evident outside the toilet too. Rajaram was familiar with it, he would pour water in the toilet after his father had used it.

Tonight, he got the same smell. Standing outside the toilet, he trembled. The smell had intensified. Rajaram entered. It was unnaturally cold inside; it wasn't supposed to be so cold. How was this possible? Rajaram had goose pimples.

He put the lamp down by the window and was about to urinate.

On his lips—

> 'He severed the heads of Ravan, not one but ten.
> But with the creator's boon they sprouted again.'

For the first time that day, Rajaram seemed to hear the splash of urine being discharged from such a short distance.

How strange! As soon as he emerged from the toilet, the smell of his father's urine vanished completely. It had begun to fade from the moment the last drop of his own urine dribbled out, and by the time he went out, it had melted into the air.

The spot where he was standing when he realized that the smell of urine had vanished was the same place where he had first encountered the smell on his way to the toilet. It was gone now. What was going on? Nothing seemed normal that night. Someone seemed intent on providing evidence of the existence of spirits. Some kind of irrefutable truth that he could not disbelieve in any circumstances. This was ominous, and Rajaram was genuinely frightened. He rushed towards his room. The punkah puller sat up with alacrity at the sound of his footsteps, gaping at his master. Rajaram hurried in without a glance at him and slammed the door loudly before locking it. Deliberately. The sound of his footsteps, of the door being slammed, gave him courage. Although Rajaram hadn't glanced at the punkah puller, his alert presence became a source of comfort at this time. The presence of the tangible within a cage of the ephemeral was reassuring.

Rajaram was filled with dread that night, the whole thing seemed supernatural. Why did the smell appear? Why did it disappear? A long time had passed since his father's death, he had not had any such experience till now. Although he did not believe in the existence of god, he did believe in the paranormal. The recent incident appeared to belong to this category. What could happen next? Would the kobiraj have to be summoned? Or a tantra practitioner? Rajaram could not fathom what was going on. At first, he made an effort to calm himself, to be steady, but suddenly he took the opposite route. As though he had been given a divine message, Rajaram now tried to rob the incident of any significance.

Eventually he succeeded. Laughing at himself, he put the recent experience at a distance from the solidity of his perceptions. As though it could now be considered nothing but an illusion. He felt serene again and rose to his feet for a drink of water. But although in his mind he had purged the incident of supernatural elements, he felt it was better to not consume too much water. What if he felt the urge to urinate again in the early hours of the morning?

Rajaram didn't indulge his thirst.

The first thought that occurred to him after he sat on his bed was that even though he had begun his unfinished letter to Dwarkanath Tagore in Bengali, he was not able to express himself properly in this language either. It was evident to him that at this preliminary stage he would not be able to personally meet the intended recipient of the letter. In Dwarkanath's presence, Rajaram's manner of speaking might appear even more incoherent than in the letter. So write he must.

Arriving at this conclusion made him restless. In a flash, he got out of bed and sat down to write his letter once again. Should he resume where he had stopped? No, he decided after some thought, he would compose an entirely new letter. The preamble would be shorter, he would abandon an excessively long introduction and go directly to the heart of the matter—the red water business enterprise. He would change the form of address in his new letter too, as well as the way he had portrayed his father.

'To

The Deeply Revered Srijukto Babu Dwarkanath Tagore

Sir

I am Srijukto Rajaram Deb. I have inherited a landed estate from my father.'

(Scratching this out, Rajaram wrote 'from my family'. This meant he would have to start the letter again on a fresh sheet of paper. About to discard the sheet he was using, Rajaram paused and continued. He'd better finish the letter here, let the mistakes appear in this version. He would write it out again without errors on another sheet of paper.)

'I have embarked on the initiative to write to you for a specific purpose. I have long harboured the desire to communicate with you, but I was unable to fulfil this wish for I did not know how to do it. After prolonged consideration I selected correspondence as the best medium. With your permission, I am writing in Bengali.

'Sir, my departed father Srijukto Debram Deb was a great admirer of yours, just as I am. Although landowners, our awareness of your various accomplishments in commerce had led my father and me to decide that we would enter the field of business in partnership with you. But his unexpected death brought our plans to a temporary halt. At present I have gathered sufficient fortitude to make an appeal to you.

'Sir, I would like to join you in the enterprise of manufacturing the alcoholic substance named rum, although I do not consume alcohol myself. I have no addictions in the truest sense of the term, I do not even smoke the hookah….'

Sleep assailed Rajaram. The corners of his eyes smarted, and the centre of his forehead throbbed. He stopped writing. He was somewhat more pleased with the form, content, and language of this version of the letter. Or so it seemed to him then. Feeling a sense of comfort, Rajaram went to bed, falling asleep instantly. And then, a dream—

A room in his house. A few familiar signs help Rajaram identify it, for he has never set eyes on the furniture he is surrounded by. They are painted a gleaming shade of silver. An unfamiliar youth lies on the bed. Starting beneath his nose, his moustache stretches downward on either side of his mouth. He holds a strange instrument, with coloured lights that blink. Something like a white string emerges from the instrument and branches into two, each branch leading to one of the youth's ears. In front of him, a canine with a white coat marked with black spots sits leaning on its forelegs, staring with its mouth wide open at the youth, who ignores its existence. The dog wags its tail from time to time, it is salivating. But it isn't clear whether it's saliva or blood—drops of a red liquid are falling from its mouth.

The half-finished letter changed its appearance the very next morning. Getting out of bed, Rajaram drew it to himself without even washing up. He no longer liked the language or the arrangement of the contents. The signs of haste when writing were evident now. What was the hurry! The choice of words was not polished, a letter like this would appear foolhardy to Dwarkanath. He might even throw it away half-read.

No, Rajaram would have to write it all over again. Slowly and steadily. It would not work otherwise.

Having eaten perfunctorily, he embarked on writing the

letter once more, this time intent on completing it. His head was crowded with thoughts, how was he to lay them out systematically?

It would take time. It would take time to compose this letter. But Rajaram wanted to arrive at the conclusion swiftly, he had no patience, though this was what he needed the most.

These reflections immediately made Rajaram despondent. He felt helpless at being thwarted in this manner, repeatedly. Why was he facing these obstacles constantly? Or were these 'obstacles' imaginary?

Latu knocked on the door. Rajaram could hear him but paid no attention, he had no wish to get to his feet. This was a regular occurrence—when he was sitting, he didn't wish to stand up, and when he was lying down, he felt no urge to sit up. He knew Latu would wait.

When he finally opened the door reluctantly, Latu told him that the cashier wished to have a conversation. He would visit Rajaram in his room if granted permission.

The mention of the cashier reminded Rajaram that he had become exceedingly irregular in checking on matters of the estate. Manohar, the cashier, was doing everything on his own. It was not right, Rajaram was wrong to be so irresponsible. It was not fitting to be disdainful about the source of his income. There was nothing he could accomplish without money.

After some thought Rajaram said, 'No need for him to come here, I'll go to the office. Tell him I will be there shortly.'

'Very well, Shaheb,' said Latu and left.

As he shut the door, Rajaram realized he had not the slightest inclination to go. He had been subjected to the same conversations, the same matters all these years. But his wealth was still limited to his family inheritance, he was unable to venture into a new world although he wished to. Was he not built then for a higher calling? Was he condemned to do nothing but maintain accounts of his landholdings as long as he lived? Would he never make any progress?

Rajaram could not find an answer. He did not know where to look for one either.

> My entire life is going to be in vain. How long can I go on in this manner? The days do not come to a halt, the days do not halt. But I have halted. Eternally. Unbearable, it is unbearable.

Despite his unwillingness Rajaram knew he would have to meet Manohar. He opened the door—to discover Krishnabhabini putting clothes out to dry on the veranda. She smiled gently at Rajaram as he stood beside the door left ajar.

> Is this how each of my days will pass?

Rajaram could not find an answer. He did not know where to look for one either.

There had been no repetition of the incident of the smell of his father's urine. He had got out of bed at midnight on two successive nights. Although he had no need to urinate, he walked towards the toilet to find out if the smell was back. Curiosity had supplanted fear, even though he knew he would be frightened all over again if he did get the smell. But he was oddly eager to feel this fear, and strange as it may seem, he felt dejected at not getting the smell anymore. At least something out of the ordinary was about to take place, but now it would not.

Stasis had invaded Rajaram, his life, his surroundings. How was he to escape? Which way lay freedom?

A year and a half passed. Nothing new took place anymore in Rajaram's life. He waited expectantly for some novelty or variety from an unknown source, and then asked himself the very next moment what it might be or could be. He had to take some steps for something new to emerge, did he not? But he had not done anything to initiate change in his listless existence.

Rajaram had left the last letter he had written to Dwarkanath Tagore incomplete. He had glanced at it every single day during the past few months, losing count of the number of times he did this. But he had been unable to add a single word.

And then one day he sat down with it again on a whim. Many scattered thoughts and ideas crowded his mind, and he wished he could write them down cogently. He decided to put them on paper as they occurred to him, later he would organize all the elements and include them in a new letter.

And so to the draft. Rajaram began to write—

'Sir I gathered information about your enterprises from my departed father. You may have wondered how I learnt of you and your activities. To assuage your curiosity, allow me to inform you that I have a neighbour by the name of Srijukto Chandramadhab Bandyopadhyay, a lawyer by profession. A copy of each and every newspaper published at present is available at his residence. Moreover, he is acquainted with many eminent personages by virtue of his profession. Accordingly, the sources and extent of his knowledge are vast. He considers me his son, and passes on all the important news to me, for I personally do not subscribe to any of the newspapers. Nor do I consort with people at large, primarily on account of the work that I am engaged in at present. To tell you the truth, my antipathy towards the aforementioned activity is also responsible. That this is not a practice to be extolled is something I am aware of.'

That day Rajaram stopped at 'I am aware of'.

Another day he wrote—

'As I informed you, I had requested my father to join you in indigo cultivation. After his demise I had decided to be a shareholder in your enterprise of manufacturing the alcoholic product named rum. At that time I was told you had recently purchased coal mines in the Raniganj area. I wish to be a partner with you in this venture. I would be gratified if you were kind enough to grant your permission. I humbly seek perpetual sanctuary under your patronage.'

In the process of placing his ruminations on the record, Rajaram could realize distinctly that his original plan had gone awry by now, he was utterly confused. Dwarkanath had proceeded with one business venture after another, while Rajaram had lost his bearings. He felt directionless, a ship unable to reach the shore. Dwarkanath was turning into a brown sahib, matching the British at every step. Everyone considered him an equal of the English masters, and even the East India Company held him in high regard. Rajaram, who lived very close to Dwarkanath, wanted to emulate him, to march to the same beat. The more Dwarkanath's temporary success grew, the more of a failure his neighbour Rajaram Deb proved to be.

It was from this time that Rajaram began to sleep completely in the nude at night. He would only have a sheet covering his body. Its touch on his skin provided him with the purest of sensations, as though it were only this moment that could bring him comfort.

And so, the days went by. Leave alone despatching the letter, Rajaram's fragmented thoughts could not even take the form of a complete missive.

Then one day Rajaram recalled something about Dwarkanath that he had heard his father say. Following the trail, he wrote—

'Sir

I request you at the outset not to condemn me. You may consider it impertinent of your servant to allow these words to escape his lips. What I am about to say is nothing but what I have heard. You must understand that for ordinary people like ourselves what we hear is the truth by another name. We do not have the means to seek confirmation of these oral narrations. Still I seek your forgiveness. I am presenting this matter to you for the sole purpose of learning the truth. When my departed father recounted to me your activities relating to your landholdings, there was one particular incident that he mentioned. You have inherited an estate in Birahimpur from your father. It appears your ryots and subjects complained to the magistrate of the aforementioned place about the ill-treatment they had received from your steward and bill collector, and secured his support. When this was brought to your attention, you threatened the magistrate with evidence of indecent incidents from his personal history and, for all intents and purposes, compelled him to withdraw his support to your subjects. In other words, you set a thief to catch a thief. Let me assure you I have no interest in the morals of the above incident. All I wish to know is whether it is true or not. I confess this has become a matter of great curiosity for me ever since.'

Drafting his letter had become something of a habit for Rajaram now. He was compelled to write something or the other constantly—some of it new, some of it old but in a newer form. Even if it was not every day, he was not particularly irregular with this activity of writing. And he seemed to have accepted that none of it would ever reach the intended recipient. And so the etiquette of correspondence and even his language became disorderly and incoherent at times. One day, for instance, on an impulse he dashed off two lines in English—

'Sir

I am not a Brahmo. Also I do not want to be a Brahmo.'

Some three years later, Rajaram learnt from Chandramadhab about an organization named the Assam Company that had been established in Assam. It would trade in tea, apparently the first corporation in the world to do so. And although the company was primarily owned by the British, two of its principal shareholders were from Calcutta: Babu Mutty Lall Seal and Babu Dwarkanath Tagore.

Although Rajaram held back his excitement at this news in Chandramadhab's presence and pretended to be his normal self, in his heart he felt everything that had been plundered from him had been restored. He had been calling on Chandramadhab, not for any particular reason, but on a whim. When he received this information, Rajaram felt his visit had been worth his effort.

It was almost evening now. Rajaram had left his residence late in the afternoon.

Yet another bend in the road, he reflected on his way back. Was Dwarkanath going to embark on every possible business in this manner? Another question occurred to Rajaram—did Dwarkanath supervise all his businesses personally? How was it possible?

But a sense of relief was taking shape in Rajaram's heart. Suddenly he was happy, for one more objective had presented itself. This time it was tea. He had to remedy the situation now. Rajaram felt invigorated and prepared to take the initiative. The old excitement had reestablished itself, emerging once more from its secret lair.

The unfinished letters of the past lay in front of him. They caught his eye every day, but he didn't touch them. The sheets were dirty, blowing on them would send up a cloud of dust which would enter his eyes and nose, making breathing difficult. Rajaram had often contemplated picking up the letters, but had kept himself from touching them even though he was tempted to. He had drawn back, musing, let them be as they are, nothing will come of it any way other than getting my hands dirty.

But one day, he found his attitude changed. That day too he was standing near the desk covered with the dusty letters. The same thought appeared initially, why disturb them, let them be. But this abstinence no longer appealed to him. Rajaram felt the urge to rummage through the sheets of paper, to write again. Dwarkanath had invested in a tea company. A tea company. Couldn't Rajaram become associated with it too, with this tea company? Wouldn't that be nice! He would also have arrangements for tea at home, he would invite people to tea—he had heard that eminent people in the city invited one another home for tea these days.

Rajaram was energized by the possibilities. Should he now write to Dwarkanath in that case? He sat down to write as thoughts coursed through his head, but jumped up immediately. Once more he sat down, once again he rose to his feet. He could not settle down, he was overcome by restlessness.

He mumbled—

'He severed the heads of Ravan, not one but ten.
But with the creator's boon they sprouted again.'

Rajaram began to pace up and down to compose himself, and then sat down clutching his hair and panting. Sitting quietly for some time, he began to read each of the drafts he had written so far. When he was done, he began writing—

'Srijukto Dwarkanath Tagore

Sir

I have not met you. I have not had the opportunity. But I confess I am deeply desirous of making your acquaintance. You could say I am impatient for it. And yet I have not found an opportunity. The responsibility is to a certain extent mine, but the environment is no less responsible. In the event of a tête-à-tête I could have explained everything to you; it is not possible to convey all of it in a letter. I have failed to arrive at a reasoned conclusion about what to include and what to omit. I am

not proficient at correspondence, I only make the effort.
I have attempted several times to write a letter to you,
even succeeding in composing a few lines each time.
But I was unable to draw any of those letters to a close,
I stopped halfway every time. How much progress can
one make in this fashion....'

As he wrote, Rajaram realized his urge to compose the letter was dying down. He was still keen to establish communication with Dwarkanath, but how was he to achieve it if he could not write, if he did not even wish to write? Who would prepare everything on his behalf?

Nothing readymade was available.

Rajaram concentrated on writing again, but it was evident that he was forcing himself.

'I have not made sufficient progress. Every letter I tried
to write remained unfinished, not even one of them
arrived at the threshold of completion. Therefore, this
fresh attempt. I will write with rapt attention, I will
convey to you everything I wish to say—I am anxious to
make you aware of them.

'Sir, despite all these thoughts I have been inactive
for a long time. My heart was not in it. But today I have
decided to take up pen and paper and write without
a pause. First, I consider it necessary to introduce
myself. I am a landowner, my name is Rajaram Deb.
Although the estate is not a source of enormous wealth
at present, my earnings from taxes are not modest. There
is no one in the family to speak of, and therefore I have
no dependents. But I am a man desirous of venturing
out, I have wanted, always, to extend myself beyond

my circumstances. I do not care to have my activities restricted. It is a matter of fate that I was born into a landowning family. But no matter, I can certainly acquire other identities, can I not? I see no obstacles. The mentality of dying a landowner because one is born a landowner is not mine. It was my father whose thoughts ran along these lines. He was unwilling to set foot in the wider world, perhaps he had no desire to or was incapable of it. I held up your exploits as an example to him many times, but still I failed to secure his permission. You too could have chosen to concentrate on a single aspect of business, but you preferred to spread yourself in various directions. This is glorious, this is a display of masculine pride. This is what is desired. But even with someone like you showing the way, what have the rest of us achieved? Precious little. We will fail, it is impossible to emulate you—these convoluted notions kept us from acting. Time passed us by, opportunities passed us by, we remained who we were, where we were. I had elaborate arguments with my father on these matters, but on each occasion we failed to arrive at a positive outcome. Even after making up my mind, I was unable to make progress. You could call it a flaw in my character.

'Still I have not given up hope of being your associate. I have repeatedly gathered the hope of writing to you, but I have not succeeded. I do not expect to get an opportunity for a meeting. Nor do I propose one. I am not given to mingling, I have no friends, I do not even leave my residence as a rule. I live behind the veil, sir. But although this has afforded me personal relief, it has caused setbacks for me everywhere on the social plane. It is as though I live in a cave, ensconced in darkness while everywhere outside is brightly illuminated. I acknowledge that much of this is by my own choice. I could have been like others if I had wanted to, but even when I attempted this, I did not succeed. I advanced part of the way, only to turn into a statue the very next moment, as though someone within me were holding me back. Try as I might, I have not been able to free myself from the serpentine coils of this invisible force. I have been silent with the knowledge that I do not wish to be silent. This may appear strange to you, as it might to anyone else. Some may even doubt my mental equilibrium. I do realize I am not entirely normal. I could have achieved a great deal, but that I did not eventually is because of my family, my environment. I myself am also responsible in no small measure, which I am not ashamed to admit. Despite all my fancies, I do not take a single step forward. Who will rectify this? How? Therefore, I am unbelievably helpless, or perhaps you could say I have ensured that I have become helpless. Anyone who came to know of this would berate me, why, I would do it myself. I do, in fact. When I am engaged in introspection, I wonder whether this is how my days, my life, my time on earth will pass. What will I have accomplished in that case? I was capable of so much, but how much did I achieve? I am a failure. A charlatan. I can talk up a storm, I think too much, I have wasted time with deleterious thoughts. If only I could have used this time, led it in the right direction, if I could have moved ahead, if I could have tried moving ahead instead of being held back by imagining failure, it could have taken me somewhere. But you can see for yourself what an imposter I am. If I have written so many things, the obvious conclusion is that I understand all these things. But even if I do, I have not acted. Whose sympathy can I expect? Everyone will say I am the architect of my own misery. Sir, it is possible I am repeating myself. I do not know if you will peruse this letter up to this point, or whether you will read it at all. Or whether this missive will even reach your hands.

'And here we are, the deleterious thoughts have returned. I was about to scratch them out with a stroke of my pen, but I did not. I did not because at the very least you will realize that pessimism is a natural trait of my personality. Sir, instead of wasting more words, let me get directly to the heart of the matter. In other words, to the mystery behind this letter. You are a well-established businessman, a successful one despite being a landowner. You do not hesitate to invest in business enterprises, you have put your money into a variety of commodities and tasted success. You have applied yourself, and you continue to apply yourself, to a succession of businesses. From the beginning I have been curious about the nature of your business ventures. I am in possession of considerable information in this respect. I have tried as much as possible with my feeble intellect to investigate your commercial efforts. And in doing so I have felt the most powerful urge to invest in business ventures just like you. I may not succeed on my own. But you are my deal, and I have made up my mind to seek your help, however difficult it may be. I will go into business in partnership with you, I will be your apprentice.

'Sir, do not condemn me, at no stage do I display the arrogance of desiring to be your equal. I wish to emulate you, in daring and in accomplishments. Such is my ambition, that is all.

'I wanted to be your associate in several of your business enterprises in the past. I began composing a series of letters in order to establish communication with you, with a view to fulfilling this objective. But there it was again. Pessimism. It has proved to be my undoing. I am unable to move forward. I am not repeating my account of the incidents of the past. Allow me to refer to your recent business venture. Tea....'

Rajaram lifted his pen from the paper at this point. He had written a great deal over several hours, putting down his thoughts as they occurred to him. He had worked up a flow of words and had decided he would review the letter only after he had finished it. He would not stop in the middle, he would not grant himself a break in writing, he would not look back. But after he had written the word 'tea' he could no longer ignore the throbbing in his head. It had begun aching some time ago, intensifying suddenly. His eyes had been streaming yesterday. Rajaram had been out of sorts for the past few days, feeling the onset of a fever and aching limbs.

Now he touched his forehead with his palm to find it warm.

Rajaram was compelled to stop writing. Lying down would bring him some relief. So he rose to his feet, only to feel his head spinning, forcing him to sit down again on the teapoy.

After some time, he lurched to the door and told the

punkah puller to call Latu. The words barely emerged from his throat, he appeared to be losing his voice.

Kedar, the vaidya, came and prescribed a couple of relevant medicines, without mentioning the cause of the fever. In response to repeated queries of 'it isn't cholera, is it?', he admonished Rajaram, 'Not at all. This illness isn't going to take you to your pyre.'

He instructed Rajaram to take long, uninterrupted rest. The vaidya was over sixty years old and bad-tempered. No one considered it wise to ask him too many questions. He didn't care for hierarchy and deferred to no one.

In any event, Rajaram's rest and recuperation were underway, and he recovered slowly. Lying in bed, he ruminated on something he had believed in since childhood—it was good to fall ill from time to time. Being confined to bed meant not being active, which in turn meant indirectly indulging idleness. It wasn't as though he was concerned with time, which he had an abundance of, but he felt he could have more of it at his disposal when he was ill. However, he was now pursued unrelentingly by another thought—would his present attempt to complete and despatch a letter to Dwarkanath also fail?

His first thought was, yes, it probably would. But then he told himself, no, his fortunes had to turn this time. He would have to find a way to complete the letter and send it to Dwarkanath. But as far as Rajaram was concerned there was nothing positive about this. Was he perpetually in search of inspiration, he wondered, in search of motivation? If that were the case, why?

A few days later he was assailed by worry again. Assume he succeeded in writing the letter and despatched it. After which it was delivered to Dwarkanath Tagore at his residence. Yet... yet what if Dwarkanath rejected it, or ignored it, giving it no importance? What would Rajaram do then? That would be the end of everything, there would no more hope. What then?

Rajaram was disconsolate. These conjecturable moments and situations threatened to nullify him and his aspirations, devastating him completely. Rajaram whirled about within a circle of fire that defeated him. Was there a way out?

Even if there was, Rajaram did not know of it. This thought gave him a perverse pleasure that led him to abandon any wish to seek an escape route. Where would such an escape lead him anyway? This too had become increasingly uncertain.

⌒

Rajaram had not completed the last letter he was writing about Dwarkanath's tea enterprise. He had neither attempted to complete it, nor begun a new draft. He had been told of Dwarkanath Tagore's first journey to England and had considered delivering a bon voyage letter in the capacity of an admirer and devotee. He would hand it over himself. But it took him no time, and no particular reason, to change his mind. A reception had been organized at the Town Hall on the eve of Dwarkanath's voyage. Despite an urge to set his eyes upon this eminent figure, Rajaram abandoned his plan at the last moment. He did not know who had been invited and who, ignored. Chandramadhab, the bearer of the news, was unable to provide more information on the list of invitees, although he had found out that a Muslim cook would be accompanying Dwarkanath to England.

Several months had passed since then. Dwarkanath was abroad. Rajaram had not gone back to the letters he had composed. That particular day he was in a pleasant mood after his bath and meal—at such times he felt he would accomplish a great deal, that he was capable of anything. Today he would count the number of letters he had drafted so far. Then he would determine the sections he could use from each of the letters to assemble a final missive. Rajaram felt enthusiastic—

He severed the heads of Ravan, not one but ten.
But with the creator's boon they sprouted again.

Gathering the letters, Rajaram lay on his stomach on his bed and began to read, counting them one by one. He had written a total of ninety-two letters in the past few years. Of course, not one of them was complete, even the last one, despite being close, had not been completed.

Winter was in the air. He was bathed in the fading sunlight coming in through the window. Suddenly Rajaram felt himself bursting with laughter, but what agony was this, he could not laugh. Unbelievable, but true. He was unable to laugh.

Heh…heh….He tried, but to no avail.

Could he only imagine an everyday act like laughing now? Was he under the impression he wanted to laugh when that was not the case at all?

A pitiful situation.

There was some space at the end of one of the drafts. Rajaram filled it with his pen.

'Sir I am slowly going mad. Things have come to a pass where I cannot laugh even if I try.'

Dwarkanath Tagore returned home in the middle of winter. He had met Queen Victoria in England, he had met the King of Belgium too. The news did not excite Rajaram, he saw no suitable reason to be inspired. In the same way, some three years later, he learnt, without enthusiasm, that Dwarkanath was on his way abroad again.

But the news he received within a year of Dwarkanath's second visit abroad did perturb him to some extent. Dwarkanath Tagore had passed away in a foreign country, his last rites had been conducted there too. He had been buried on foreign soil, like his friend Ram Mohan Roy.

It was as though this was what Rajaram had been waiting for. Death. Dwarkanath Tagore's death. As though he had succeeded in breaking free of his incompleteness, of his failure. There was nothing more to be done, no one to write to, no approval or permission to seek, no partnership to enter into. What could not be concluded, even when it had ended, had finally been extirpated, complete with its roots—this too was cause for elation.

On a blank sheet of paper, Rajaram wrote, even though it was of no use whatsoever—

'Babu Srijukto Dwarkanath Tagore

I heard you have died....'

Here he stopped to scratch out the word 'died' and replace it with 'passed away', only to reflect, who's going to look at it anyway? This was all he wrote before tucking the sheet into the pile of earlier drafts. But he had an urge to write more. It appeared he had been emboldened to ask Dwarkanath some probing questions, things Rajaram could not have said in Dwarkanath's lifetime. What was it he wished to write?

He wished to ask—

Sir, you went into business in partnership with white men, did they acknowledge and respect you as a genuine shareholder? Did they consider you their equal? I also wish to know, I am told not all your business ventures were successful, what was the reason for those enterprises to fail? Was it you, or was it your courtiers? Did you not have the time to supervise everything yourself? Is it true that there was a significant lack of organizational ability?

No, Rajaram did not eventually write any of this. Had his infatuation ended? Just as Dwarkanath had tried to match steps with the Englishmen and failed on the brink of success, Rajaram too had tried to emulate Dwarkanath and work in proximity with him, only to fail eventually.

Rajaram was struck by anxiety—what if his personal failure spread like an epidemic across all of Bengal?

But this possibility did not worry him very long. By then, his curiosity and inclinations had taken a different turn.

There was a tiny coop beside the stairs leading to the terrace, home to discarded things which no one had touched in years. They were covered in dust and never cleaned.

Rajaram used to enjoy spending time on the roof, but now he no longer felt a longing to go there. Still, his heart felt lighter when he did climb up to the roof, as though he had arrived in an open space from a confined one.

One afternoon, as Rajaram was on his way up there, his eyes happened to fall on the coop covered in dust. He paused and then sat down on the stairs to rummage through whatever was within reach. Dust began to fly, caking his fingers, its smell was evident. Holding his breath, he scoured the pile. One rejected object after another—old crockery, flower vases, candle stands, glass ornaments.

Then something wrapped in cloth appeared in view. It had been lying at the bottom of a pile, only becoming visible after the other things had been moved. The cover had turned loose, the knot was all but undone, as though whatever lay inside was forcing its way out. Or trying to.

Rajaram leaned forward and began to unwrap the package with mounting interest.

What emerged were books. Two of them. He had never seen one of them, while the other was one his tutor, Manmatha, had given him to read in his adolescence. Rajaram didn't even remember that his tutor had not reclaimed the book, although he couldn't recollect the reason.

The two books were similar, both were dictionaries. The unknown one was entirely in English. The binding had unravelled and the cover was missing, as were the opening entries. Only some of the words from A to C remained. Neither the title nor the ownership of the dictionary could be identified.

The second one, his tutor's, was in relatively better condition, although this one was also slightly torn. It was an English-to-Bengali dictionary composed by a White missionary from Serampore. Its title:

ABRIGMENT of JOHNSON'S DICTIONARY

ENGLISH AND BENGALI.

PECULIARLY CALCULATED

FOR THE USE of EUROPEAN AND NATIVE STUDENTS.

By JOHN MENDIES

Considering the vortex of mystery around the objects as they revealed themselves gradually to Rajaram, the scene would have found an appropriate climax had they turned out to be immensely valuable. Naturally, no one else would have been delighted to discover only these tattered volumes after so much effort. But to Rajaram this was a positively thrilling event—the recovery of these two books was like retrieving hidden treasure. It put him in a positively breezy state of mind. With the air of a man infinitely pleased, Rajaram went towards his room with the books. Indistinctly, he muttered, 'He severed the heads of Ravan, not one but ten. But with the creator's boon they sprouted again.'

Climbing down the stairs, he wondered why he had been on his way to the roof in the first place. Was there a reason or an objective? Or was it just a casual decision? He could not remember, his mind was blank.

Rajaram began to read the two dictionaries turn by turn from that day onwards. So many words, such a variety of meanings. A wealth of Bengali words conveying new feelings whose English equivalent he did not know, or even felt the need to know. But how marvellous it was to learn them now, in this manner.

Rajaram was overcome by ecstasy as he journeyed through this acquisition of knowledge.

Amongst all these words was one that attracted him greatly. This one word seemed to have acquired a corporeal form, become a living entity. He could not fathom the reason for this outlandish obsession with a single word. Was it the sound, or was it the difference in the way it had been written in the two dictionaries? Like the lines from Kashidas, Rajaram kept uttering the word repeatedly. An English word. Carnival.

PART TWO

'We live, as we dream—alone….'

—Joseph Conrad

'…there are but a handful of stories in the world; and if the young are to be forbidden to prey upon the old then they must sit for ever in silence.'

—J. M. Coetzee

FIVE

Slowly the sky grew lighter. There was a touch of crimson in the eastern corner of the blue canopy. Dawn was on its way.

The appointed hour.

Might they arrive anytime now? So they had said. At some point of time they would be here.

When would that be? Was it not time yet? When was the much-awaited ultimate carnival to start?

They would come, wouldn't they?

Rajaram moved his hands from the pile of letters. No, he didn't know whether Dwarkanath had witnessed the carnival. His hands had become dirty. Smooth black specks of dust on his palm.

> The other day too, my palms and fingers had become dusty, in the very same manner. That day, when I retrieved those two books from the coop beside the staircase.

Rajaram rubbed his hands on his shawl with great force. Black marks appeared on it.

Simantini had fallen asleep again. She did not realize it wouldn't do for her to be asleep. She simply had to remain awake. About to rouse her, Rajaram paused. He would wake her up when they were here, he decided, or perhaps she would awaken on her own at their arrival.

Rajaram no longer felt sleepy or even drowsy. But now that the hour was here, his vigil and excitement and curiosity might end any moment. His patience seemed to snap every now and then. He did try to get hold of himself the very next moment, but he could no longer contain his restlessness.

He alternated between bursting into laughter as he gripped the teapoy and sitting on the bed, gazing at the window with a woebegone expression. And sometimes he muttered the lines, 'He severed the heads of Ravan, not one but ten. But with the creator's boon they sprouted again.'

At intervals, his eyes drifted to two books stacked one below the other on his desk—the tattered English dictionary of unknown name, and J. Mendies's English-to-Bengali dictionary.

Each of the volumes was open on a specific page with the help of a carved, medium-sized ivory tusk bookmark. A particular word was circled with ink on each of the pages.

The word was 'carnival'.

Every now and then Rajaram uttered the word beneath his breath, as though speaking to himself. 'Carnival.'

SIX

It was morning, but difficult to tell how many hours had passed since dawn. The sunlight had disappeared. It was grey everywhere, the sky covered by thick clouds, their bodies plump. From time to time, they were lit up in a purple glow by snaking flashes of lightning. Low rumbles could be heard. A cold, rain-scented breeze blew erratically, punctuated by gusts of stormy wind that swept fallen leaves up in the air. Dust blew in too, flying around.

Rajaram could hear drum beats similar to the ones heard during the ritual worship of the goddess Durga. Faint at first, they grew louder gradually. It was clear that the drummers did not number half a dozen, it was the collective sound of more than a hundred drums. Conch shells were being blown in between. The sounds came from downstairs.

Leaving his room, Rajaram walked slowly out to the veranda and leant over the balustrade for a glimpse. But he could see nothing.

What was going on? What was the source of these sounds? It was clear that the notes of this colossal festivities rose from somewhere below him. Why then could he not see anything? Was it all in his head? Or had some invisible power blocked his vision?

An invisible power. The very thought was astonishing. When had he started believing in invisible powers?

No, he might as well go downstairs himself to find out. It was impossible that nothing was going on in the house. But what could it be? Who could have come in here? Why this grand arrangement?

Rajaram experienced a sudden spasm of fear. He felt his entire body tremble. His skin prickled.

He also realized by then that he was on his way downstairs.

Rajaram climbed down the stairs slowly towards the thakurdalan. He felt like a stranger in his own home—unable to fathom the reason for the festivities. Eventually when he arrived, Latu and Shashi were nowhere to be seen.

But the scene!

Drummers all around, playing on their drums madly. How many of them in all? Fifty? Sixty? Or a hundred? No, an unaccountably large number. More than a thousand drummers were gathered here. Was this even possible? How could it be possible?

At the extremity of every drum silky white bird feathers were attached, waving like flags. The drummers' faces had a strange appearance, covered in layers of white paint like those of clowns. The corners of their eyes had been elongated by lines of paint stretching to their ears.

Accompanying them on conch shells were an almost equal number of women, young and middle-aged. Did Rajaram know any of them? No...no...he didn't know any of them. Who were they? All of them were dressed in white saris with red borders. Their long, wet hair hung loose, they wore vermilion in the parting of their hair. Their soles were lined with red, they had gold ornaments on their arms and wrists, as well as the shell bangles worn by married women. Thick golden necklaces too. Like the drummers, their faces were also covered in layers of white paint. Many of the women stood next to Rajaram now; but how strange, they seemed oblivious to his presence.

Suddenly Rajaram saw a stream of blood-red water flowing in from a corner at furious speed. A torrent of water splashing into the courtyard, filling it with a red liquid. Was this water or blood? Where had it come from?

The drum beats grew louder. The drummers became even more euphoric. Some of them began to dance, gradually several others followed suit, and finally, all of them. It was impossible to them how many people there were. A thousand or more. They seemed to be all over the house, in all the nooks and crannies too, as though they had taken their positions long ago and were fully prepared for the occasion. They had begun playing their drums and conch shells when the time came. As though each of them had been born in a single moment from someone else's body and emerged from it.

The women matched the quickening beat of the drums by regulating their breathing and blowing on their conch shells even louder. It had begun to rain. Claps of thunder could be heard at intervals. The courtyard was now flooded with red water. Blood water. Raindrops collided loudly with it. Water hitting water. Rajaram could hear everything. So many things were unfolding in his house and yet he could say nothing about any of it, he couldn't ask anyone any questions. He appeared paralysed. Even in these dreadful surroundings he was seemingly an immobile spectator. The hair on his skin stood on end, but still Rajaram was dumbfounded. He was himself astounded by this vision.

Some of the women had stopped blowing on their conch shells and begun to ululate.

But why? What was being celebrated? What was all this?

The echoes of the drums, conch shells, and ululation reverberated throughout the house.

In the sky, the rain, and the clouds, and the thunder told a story....

This was the point at which Rajaram woke up. Even without glancing at the clock he knew it was almost mid-morning. As he jerked upright and jumped out of bed, the dream reasserted itself in his mind. In his waking state, the incidents in it alarmed him even more. What was this chain of incomprehensible events! Not that the presence of the fantastic was unusual in his dreams, but even by those standards this was an unprecedented novelty.

'Just like a carnival,' Rajaram soliloquized. It had become a habit for him now to utter the word carnival frequently.

It was the first day of the English new year. A new decade had begun. The fifties. The Britishers had caroused late into the night, the sounds of their celebrations were heard everywhere. Their part of the city was up till dawn. Rajaram had decided to go for a stroll by the river today. Near Eden Gardens, he would feast his eyes on the attire of the Englishwomen and Englishmen. Rajaram enjoyed going for walks and watching people, especially the British—their clothes, their behaviour. These days he hardly ever went out, his heart wasn't in it. But today he had the urge.

Rajaram grew cheerful as soon as the idea occurred to him. He tried not to brood about his dream anymore. Wrapping his shawl around himself, he rose to his feet, opened the windows, and held out his hands to the warmth of the sun. Closing his eyes, he tried to feel the presence of the sunbeams on his eyelids. They were gathered there collectively, he could feel their weight. His eyeballs moved, and at matching speed he could see blackish-green shadows—spherical, rectangular, so many different forms. One shape changing into another, then disintegrating. Melting. Flowing like waves. And at times darkness flashed, behind it a clear ring of light.

But the evening stroll didn't materialize. The closer it came to the time to leave, the more hesitant Rajaram became. For he knew the British behaved most rudely and boorishly with Indians in that part of the city. They didn't even spare the rich babus, they humiliated anyone dressed in Indian attire around Eden Gardens.

Rajaram himself had never got off his carriage over there, he had always driven through it. He had only heard about these things from Chandramadhab, one of whose acquaintances had been made to suffer in this manner.

This reminded Rajaram that Chandramadhab was ill. He had retired from his legal practice quite some time ago because of old age. His son, Nabinmadhab, had donned his father's mantle and had built a reputation as a lawyer.

In any event, the threat of being assaulted by Englishmen made Rajaram think twice before going for a walk. It was, moreover, their new year. Who knew what exploits they were capable of.

> These white men are proving to be pests. Why can't you go back to your own country, why do you have to swagger about in ours!

Apparently, it was impossible to venture out towards Kidderpore in the evening. White sailors from the ships lined the streets and robbed Indian passengers and passers-by of all their possessions. The babus of the city were perpetually terrified of them.

Eventually Rajaram abandoned the luxurious idea of an evening promenade. It did occur to him that he could always go down to the river, but the very next moment, he decided not to go out at all.

Krishnabhabini had said she would go too. They would have taken the phaeton. The coachman and the groom were waiting. The horse could be heard neighing and stamping its feet. Because of the reduction in the number of excursions, the staff in charge of the coach and the horse barely had any work these days. Rajaram had even considered dispensing with a personal carriage. Since he almost never went out, the coachman and the groom might as well be fired. He would see what to do if the need to go out ever arose.

But Rajaram did not act on his thoughts. Let them be as they were. It was just a matter of a single phaeton. When he was still desirous of an audience with Dwarkanath, the need for a carriage was on his mind—a businessman-landowner without a carriage of his own was unacceptable, so he had to keep his coach. But with that desire having ended, he no longer spared a thought for his personal transportation.

The coachman and the groom were in an enthusiastic frame of mind today, at last they had some work on their hands. But Rajaram informed them through Latu that he wouldn't be going out after all.

He was unhappy about having to tell Krishnabhabini. Ever since his aunt's death, the responsibility for Krishnabhabini's well-being had been Rajaram's. He had to shoulder it whether he wanted it or not, there was no choice. But it was not particularly burdensome, for the young woman lived independently, without imposing on him. So even though he was a trifle perturbed about it at first, Rajaram didn't worry about it too much subsequently, as though it made no difference whether he had taken the responsibility for looking after Krishnabhabini or not.

'I'm not going after all today, Bini, I know I'd told you I'd go. But then it occurred to me there might be trouble today, so you know....'

'Oh…all right.'

Rajaram tried to prolong the conversation to make things lighter. 'It's becoming troublesome to live in the city. Hundreds of foreigners…their numbers keep going up. The Englishmen were here already and now look at what's going on in Mechhuabazar—Africans have settled there. I keep hearing of brawls and murders. Can you imagine? It's all a carnival, a carnival.'

Krishnabhabini's reaction was unchanged. Rajaram considered such severity unjustified. But even though he was irked, he comprehended the situation and restrained himself from expressing his annoyance.

'We'll go another day Bini, very soon.'

'All right,' said Krishnabhabini and left.

A little later she could be heard singing in her room.

As he told Krishnabhabini about the Africans in Mechhuabazar, Rajaram began thinking about Dwarkanath. The Tagore residence was in Mechhuabazar. After Dwarkanath's death his son, Debendranath, had taken charge. It was said that all the business enterprises Dwarkanath had set up had either been wound down or were in trouble. The Carr-Tagore Company, the Union Bank, all of these were things of the past.

The information felt lifeless when it reached Rajaram. He experienced nothing—neither excitement or relief nor pain.

All he had told himself, 'It's just the carnival, that's all.'

⁂

'Carnival'. Of the hundreds of familiar and unfamiliar words in the entire dictionary, it was difficult to say what special, hidden element of this word could attract anyone's attention or curiosity. But it was this one word, just the one, that drew Rajaram irresistibly. He did not know the reason behind it, nor did he try to decipher it. For he had no wish to find out. Still, he felt there was something unique concealed in the word, as though it was about to tell him something. Or that it was waiting for an opportunity to tell everyone. A communicative word.

A word you could make friends with. 'Carnival'.

The meaning of the word in the tattered dictionary with no name was given as:

> 'Carnival—n.f [carnaval—Fr] The feaſt held in the popiſth countries before Lent—a time of luxury.'

Below this was a quote:

> 'The whole year is but one mad carnival–and we are voluptuous not ſo much upon deſire or appetite—as by way of exploit and bravery—Causes of the Decay of Christian Piety.'

John Mendies was the reader and director of the Serampore Mission Press. In the English-to-Bengali dictionary he had compiled, the meaning of the word was given in one sentence—'the special period before the Lent fast'. This dictionary used to belong to Rajaram's tutor, who had given it to Rajaram to read. There was something Rajaram still remembered in this context—handing him the dictionary, Manmatha had said, 'Look at the name, it is based on a famous English dictionary. An abridged edition. The compiler has selected some of the words from the original English dictionary and explained them in Bengali for us. Do you understand?'

Rajaram nodded.

Then Manmatha said, 'As you can see, the name tells you the title of the original, which was Samuel Johnson's *A Dictionary of the English Language*. Do you know who Samuel Johnson was?'

'No.'

'Dr Samuel Johnson was a renowned English scholar. The finest compiler of an English language dictionary in modern times.'

What an adolescent Rajaram learnt that evening from Manmatha, whose face glistened with sweat in the light from the castor oil lamp, astonished him. There was an entire world beyond the one he had seen and heard and known so far. How close could he get to it? How deeply could he enter it?

Even if it seemed a trivial matter, sometimes even an insignificant thing assumes an extraordinariness, evoking wonder without any obvious reason. The above-mentioned incident occupied just such a place in Rajaram's heart, it felt effervescent.

In any event, Rajaram could not comprehend the difference in the meaning of the two words in the two dictionaries. Even the first meaning given in the English dictionary had proved beyond his reach. Although he did not know the precise meaning of Lent, he had arrived at a superficial understanding of the word from the Bengali dictionary. There was a practice of fasting named Lent, a period before which was known as the Carnival. But when it came to 'a time of luxury', Rajaram found his way blocked. There was no elucidation of this term in the Bengali dictionary. What exactly was Lent, and what was this time of luxury before it? Was it a time of genuine indulgences, or was it a holy day of some kind? If the latter, that would make it religious.... Was he confusing things? Why should there be luxury before a religious ceremony?

Although Rajaram was unable to break through the barrier of his initial doubt and penetrate the mystery of the meaning, the word 'carnival' sent out its roots and planted itself in his brain, manifesting itself on his tongue—'A carnival, all of it'; 'This was a carnival'. It had become his private or public response to a variety of incidents. Sometimes he would yell, 'Carnival!' and shrink with embarrassment the next moment. Gayaram, the punkah puller, would often be startled outside his room on hearing such cries.

Although he uttered the word now and then in Krishnabhabini's presence, she never asked him about it at first. Later, she did.

No one else posed a question about it even if they heard. But then not too many people witnessed him saying it, for Rajaram had all but stopped going out. The management of the estate was delegated entirely to the cashier and revenue collector. Gradually he had even ceased his inspections. Rajaram would visit Chandramadhab at home one or two times every month, but he had little doubt in his mind about which of the two—to exchange pleasantries or to glean information—he went for.

The year passed as before, perhaps dictated by precedent. Nothing new took place. Sometimes Rajaram marvelled that life could go on in this fashion. An impossible stasis flowing through time.

One morning, Latu brought a letter. It was from Chandramadhab. Latu stood by after handing over the letter, as though he wished to say something once Rajaram had read the letter.

It was an invitation. Babu Kasiprasad Ghosh, an eminent personage of Calcutta, would be dining at Chandramadhab's residence tonight, and Rajaram's presence was requested on the occasion.

Kasiprasad Ghosh was a renowned man. He had already acquired considerable fame as a student of Hindu College. An expert scholar of English and its literature. His hold over the language was unparalleled. He was the first Bengali poet in the English language, with several volumes of his poetry having been published. He had also published articles in various newspapers and was the editor of the *Hindu Intelligencer*. He had a presence in official papers too. Rajaram knew this already, so the invitation afforded him both joy and enthusiasm. He told Latu, 'I will not be eating at home tonight. Chandramadhab Babu has invited me to dinner.'

It was evident from Latu's expression that even if he was not prepared for this news, it had pleased him. He appeared much more relaxed on seeing his employer looking cheerful, even if slightly, after a long time.

'Very well, Shaheb,' said Latu, and then, about to continue, paused hesitantly.

'Was there anything else?'

'Just that…if you could give us a day off tomorrow. Shashi

and I have to go...to Ghoshpaara...we'll be back before the evening.'

'Ghoshpaara? What for? Isn't that where the Kartabhaja people live?'

'Yes, Shaheb, that's where we're going. There will be singing.'

Rajaram had always considered the Kartabhajas nothing but low class, low-caste people. Apparently, the neighbourhood was a den of thugs and whores. To Rajaram, it seemed most unsuitable for his domestic retainers to be going to a musical performance organized by the very same Kartabhajas. Then he reflected, while he could always say no, would that be fitting? Why bother so much, it was a matter of half a day, let them do as they pleased, what did he care?

'Yes, all right. You may go.'

Latu had begun to fret at his employer's long silence. He had assumed he would not get permission. But Rajaram's positive response after the pause pleased him greatly. But would Rajaram eat, then?

'I will make all the arrangements and tell the maid to come and cook for you in the morning and evening. You know her, Shaheb, Chiteyr Maa.'

Chiteyr Maa, as everyone called her because her son was known as Chitey, was an elderly woman who sold flowers by the Chitreshwari temple. She lived nearby and had been frequenting this house from Rajaram's father's time to supply flowers. But she had not been here of late. There was no need.

'Of course, I know her.' However, Rajaram was not keen on having her come here and cook. 'But there's no need to ask her. I'll tell Bini, she will cook. It's not a big task. You can go. Come back on time, that's all.'

'Selaam, Shaheb,' said Latu several times and was about to

leave when Rajaram called out to him.

'Shaheb...?'

'Yes, this is what I called out to you for. Tell me, we refer to the white people, the Company officers, as Shaheb. Britishers, all of them, their skins are different from ours. But why do you call me Shaheb? Even Babu...you could call me Korta Moshai too.'

Latu had no idea how to answer this question. That there could even be such a question was beyond his understanding of the world. He only stood there with a vapid smile.

Rajaram had another question. That is to say, the question had sprung into his head at that very moment. Without considering whether it was reasonable for him to ask this, and without waiting for an answer to his previous query, he blurted out, 'Why don't Shashi and you have any children?'

Latu was caught unaware. After a short silence, he said, 'Long story, Shaheb. Shashi says she doesn't want children. Says she's barren. Won't let me anywhere near her.' The last statement seemed to have escaped him without warning, embarrassing him. Getting a hold of himself, he continued softly, 'I am with Shashi after her husband died. Shashi is in fact a widow. I am her companion. We didn't get married.'

Rajaram was nonplussed. He had never heard of such a thing before. A widow living with another man. Without even marrying him. How peculiar. Rajaram had heard that the Sanskrit scholar Vidyasagar was fighting for widows to be allowed to remarry. He was reviled by many people in the city for this, and meanwhile, just look at what was going on here.

Rajaram had seen Shashi and Latu working here at home for years together. They had joined at the same time, and while his father was alive, they had become the principal house staff. It had never occurred to Rajaram that they might not be married to each other.

Latu could surmise Rajaram's astonishment from his expression. To make light of the matter, he said, 'This is us lower-class people doing dirty things, Shaheb, that's all. You know what they say, build a house, let goats come in; be a whore; let everyone in.'

Latu chuckled.

'May I go now, Shaheb?'

'Yes.'

Rajaram was elated when he heard of the special guest expected at the dinner. At first he couldn't identify the reason for his delight, but it became clear to him afterwards. He was positively ecstatic—Kasiprasad Ghosh was someone whom Rajaram could ask for the precise meaning of the word 'carnival'. He was bound to provide an authentic answer, for which he was qualified. Finally, after all these years, Rajaram's doubts would be dispelled. He felt excitement bubbling up within himself, as though his fortune was about to turn.

'There will be a carnival. Ah.... He severed the heads of Ravan, not one but ten. But with the creator's boon they sprouted again.' Rajaram went up to the mirror and stood in front of it. As though he was observing himself. A little later, he began to hum the beat of the holy dance performed with an earthen lamp for the deities, intently swaying his arms and body to the rhythm.

Babu Kasiprasad Ghosh was a handsome man. A slim moustache above his upper lip drooped on either side of his mouth. His drowsy eyes were impossibly clever. His clothes were elegant, and he wore a round turban on his head. Rajaram estimated they were about the same age, he acknowledged that the man had a distinct personality and was worthy of respect.

Unnecessarily long preparations had delayed Rajaram's arrival. He begged everyone's pardon for being late as he entered. But his behaviour suggested that although he had been invited by Chandramadhab, it was the chief guest Kasiprasad whose forgiveness he sought for his tardiness.

Chandramadhab introduced him to Kasiprasad.

An unusual matter was being discussed when Rajaram joined the guests. Soon he grasped what it was. A revolt had taken place in the Santhal region, whose inhabitants had turned against the Company and local landowners. Two Santhals, Sidhu and Kanu, were the leaders of the movement. The Company was in trouble, and the landowners were alarmed as well.

Kasiprasad was a knowledgeable man. His conversation revealed that his learning came not just from books but also from experience. He talked about the hatred and contempt that the urban people harboured for Santhals and how this had complicated matters for them, so that their war was now being fought against two sets of people. 'Neither we nor they realize this. Whoever seizes their land, whoever deprives them of their land, is their enemy, be they foreigners or Indians. This must be appreciated.'

Rajaram listened in silence. He had nothing to contribute.

> I keep listening all the time. Rajaram listens. I don't speak. No one is waiting to hear what I have to say. No one wants to hear me. I am Rajaram Deb.

Chandramadhab interjected now and then with more information to take the discussion further. But although

Rajaram knew his presence at such a gathering was nothing but physical, he enjoyed it greatly. A distinct joy brewed within him, since he would soon learn what a carnival was and what it had meant originally. And the person who would enlighten him was standing in front of him. Rajaram had jotted down the meanings he had found in the dictionary on a piece of paper and brought it along.

Even suppressing happiness brings its own pleasure. This was the pleasure Rajaram was immersed in now.

It was after a long wait that Rajaram finally found an opportunity. The introductions had been made already; what Rajaram had been seeking was some privacy. Finally, the moment presented itself. There were other guests, of course, but no one nearby. Kasiprasad had just emerged from the toilet. Rajaram had been hovering outside the door when he saw Kasiprasad go in. As soon as he came out, Rajaram went up to him and said, 'There was something I wanted to talk to you about.'

'Of course, do tell me.'

Rajaram surveyed the surroundings quickly. Many of the guests were busy eating. The host was not nearby either.

'I have something to ask you. You are a great expert in the English language, which is why I consider it fitting to seek an answer from you. If you please…what is the correct meaning of the English word "carnival"? I have long been trying to arrive at the accurate meaning. I have not got around to asking anyone. I mean, I do not know how to bring this up with anyone. I was considering asking Chandramadhab Babu when his invitation presented itself. And I found you. So, if you would be kind enough to….'

Rajaram held up the piece of paper he had brought. Pointing to what he had written on it, he said, 'I have an ancient, tattered dictionary, entirely in English. It is impossible anymore to find out its title…such is its condition. So, this is what it says in that dictionary. And here, the meaning given below is from the Bengali dictionary compiled by the Serampore missionary John Mendies. They don't appear identical to me. Hence, the question….'

Kasiprasad glanced at the piece of paper. Then he said, 'Hmm…. The carnival is related to Christianity, primarily. Just like the French origin of the word you see here, there is a Latin term too, carna vale, farewell to meat. Anyhow, you see this reference to Lent pertains to the time before Easter, when Jesus was resurrected….' After a pause, Kasiprasad asked Rajaram, 'I presume you are familiar with the life of Jesus Christ.'

Manmatha Babu had told him the story of Jesus. Rajaram conveyed this innocently to Kasiprasad, an innocence that brought a smile to the listener's face. He returned to what he was saying, the smile intact. 'Yes…. So, the day Christ was resurrected is known as Easter Sunday. Six weeks before Easter is Lent, when Christians are supposed to eat vegetarian food. The period is dedicated to the memory of the forty days Jesus spent in the forest. And the period just before Lent is the Carnival. A brief immersion into wild revelry before entering a phase of self-restraint. But over time any huge festival came to be known as a carnival. I trust I have been able to explain.'

Rajaram listened in rapt attention. He was enjoying this thoroughly. No one had ever explained anything to him in this manner. Had he for that matter ever been in the company of such a learned person? Never.

Dwarkanath…. Dwarkanath…. There could have been such an association.

'Oh yes, most certainly,' Rajaram answered, dripping gratitude. Then he said, 'But there is one additional meaning in the English dictionary which is missing from the Bengali one. This is where I'm confused. Why this difference?'

Kasiprasad did not pay much attention to this matter. 'Nothing important, Rajaram, compiled by a missionary, after all...so he omitted the bit about the revelry,' he laughed. 'By the way,' he added, 'The English dictionary you are referring to, well, having read this entry I am sure it's Dr Johnson's *Dictionary of the English Language*. Where did you get it?'

Although the acquisition of Dr Johnson's dictionary in threadbare condition was a matter of bewilderment for Rajaram, he told Kasiprasad how it had come into his hands.

'I see,' said Kasiprasad. And then, as though his analysis so far had been meagre, he exclaimed, 'Simply put, the word carnival means immeasurable ecstasy.'

'Immeasurable ecstasy?'

'Yes, celebrations whose intensity cannot be estimated. But tell me something, Rajaram, of all the words in the dictionary why are you so interested in this one in particular?'

Rajaram seemed to have a readymade answer. 'I ask myself the same question, Kasiprasad Babu, I wonder about it too.'

This was where the conversation ended that night. It was quite late by the time the dinner ended. The guests left at last, as did Rajaram.

Rajaram pondered over several things on his way back home and even after he had returned. He didn't know whether he would meet Kasiprasad ever again, but he had experienced deep satisfaction tonight. A memorable night. And what had lodged itself permanently in his consciousness was 'immeasurable ecstasy'.

So a 'carnival' was immeasurable ecstasy. There would be a carnival, there would be ecstasy, there would be immeasurable ecstasy. Rajaram repeated this to himself a countless number of times, with a smile playing on his face. As though he had found what he was seeking. The treasure he had been searching high and low was within reach now.

Rajaram went to bed that night in a pleasant frame of mind. Just the one thing remained unknown—how did Dr Johnson's dictionary end up with him and why in this ripped-up state? Who had torn it apart?

Rajaram felt he would never have an answer.

Soon he was overcome by sleep.

Chandramadhab died within a year. He had been ailing for a long time, his kidneys had stopped working. To Rajaram this death amounted to the death of his acquisition of knowledge. Chandramadhab's son, Nabinmadhab, was not like his father. Who would keep Rajaram informed now? How would he know what was going on in the world outside?

He was not in the habit of subscribing to newspapers or reading them. Should he get a newspaper at home then? There were several to choose from. It was just a matter of getting someone to fetch one for him every day.

Let us see, let us see.

Rajaram also found it strange that instead of mourning the death of someone he had known for such a long time, he was filled with regret because he would no longer receive news of people and the country. Was he becoming selfish?

Am I growing selfish or was I always selfish? Which, Rajaram, which?

Rajaram had heard that the Company had passed the Widow Remarriage Act. He had visited Chandramadhab to learn the details. As it happened, it turned out to be their last meeting. That was when Chandramadhab had given Rajaram some astonishing news. Gas lights were going to be installed on the streets of the city. Perhaps very soon. Beginning with Chowringhee, where the British lived.

Many eminent people visited Chandramadhab's residence, and one of them had informed him of this development. The comment he had added kept ringing in Rajaram's ears—'Our black town, Rajaram, will become blacker, it will get much darker here.'

Taking the shawl hanging near the head of the bed and wrapping it around himself, Rajaram paced up and down, reflecting on these developments. Pausing, he sat down on the bed and stretched his limbs, took a sip of water, and then opened the door to call out, 'Latu, bring the lamp.'

He was about to retreat into his room immediately afterwards when it seemed to him he could see a glow in the yard. Who could be there now, what were they up to? Going out to the veranda, he saw Krishnabhabini arranging lamps in a circle in the middle of the courtyard and then lighting them. Oh, of course! It was the night of Bhoot Chaturdashi. Very well then.

A little later Rajaram went downstairs too.

Krishnabhabini's face and neck were lit by the lamps. Her cleavage was conspicuous. Her skin was a tempting and open expanse, an invitation for unrestricted exploration. Rajaram felt his blood pounding; he was overwhelmed by an indescribable urge to which he was deeply desirous of surrendering his body. He had never experienced such a sensation before—what was this he was feeling today? He was not remotely prepared for such an experience. The situation demanded that he do something, but what? He couldn't tell. What could he possibly do now?

'He severed the heads of Ravan, not one but ten....'

'I want to hear you sing today, Bini, it's the night of Bhoot Chaturdashi, a real carnival.'

⁘

Two months had passed after Krishnabhabini's death. It was the twilight hour between the end of winter and the beginning of spring. Rajaram lay in his own room one evening with a slight headache. The window was open, with a gentle breeze wafting in. Although it was largely pleasant, Rajaram felt chilly now and then. After a long time had passed this way, he decided to shut the windows. But he simply had no wish to get out of bed, as was usually the case with him.

It was five past seven on the clock. He usually ate his dinner an hour later, but even the thought, that is to say, the thought of eating, made him nauseous. Rajaram tossed and turned before lying on his stomach and rubbing his eyes against the bedclothes. At intervals, he lay spreadeagled.

This was the position he was in when the door to his room burst open with a loud noise, even though it was locked. Terrified by the sound and the unexpectedness, Rajaram shot upright and sat staring in that direction with a hammering heart. Had the door broken or something, considering how loud the sound was?

No, the door was neither broken nor damaged. But the sight that confronted Rajaram numbed his judgement, making it impossible to choose between screaming and resisting. His limbs were paralysed in an instant.

Simantini had been sitting quietly in a corner. Unaccountably frightened, she dashed off to hide beneath the bed without even a look at anything around her.

Rajaram saw that, far from being broken, the door had not even opened, it was closed, as before. But miraculously, someone had entered, like a magician—a man dressed entirely in western clothes. He was lean, but eye-catchingly tall. On his head was a bowler hat, the kind Europeans wore. Half his face was hidden in his shadow. His coat hung below his knees, and his feet were shod in pointed boots. In his hand he held a cane. The man walked in arrogantly.

Even more astonishingly, he was not alone. He had a companion. This follower had just entered: a gigantic, adjutant stork. It was following the man with slow, dignified footsteps. There was an angry look in the bird's blazing eyes. It fluttered its wings twice, violently, with a deafening sound.

Who are they? Who are they!

The European went up to Rajaram's teapoy. The adjutant stork walked past Rajaram to the window and stood there gazing outside with a most annoyed expression. Their routes and positions seemed predetermined.

Rajaram watched them in utter amazement. In his hurry to jump out of bed he had stubbed his right foot against the wooden footboard. The pain in his toes proved that he wasn't dreaming. Rajaram even got a whiff of the stork's odour as the bird walked past him.

No, this is not a dream. But what is it if not a dream?
What a strange scene is unfolding before my eyes.

He did not appear to have anything to say. Not a word on his lips. Not a sentence made of words. What was going on? Who were they? How did they get in? The locked door wasn't broken. And yet they had entered so easily.

What were Latu and Shashi doing? And Simantini? Oh right, she was beneath the bed. The punkah puller? No, he wasn't here now.

Rajaram could see no opportunity to question the intruders. He was unable to utter a sound, and his limbs were frozen. He could not tell whether to get out of bed or stay there. Rajaram had wanted to block the adjutant stork from entering, but to no avail. He lacked the strength to get to his feet. And now a bird that ate garbage was inside his room, even though its behaviour suggested it had come in reluctantly, under compulsion.

The European aroused fear. His face wasn't visible, but it was clear his eyes were boring into Rajaram.

Silence reigned for some time.

Then it was the man who broke it.

'Are you quite done with being frightened and astonished? I am…that is to say we are…waiting.'

Rajaram had no idea how to respond. The European was speaking idiomatic Bengali.

Gulping, he asked in a quivering voice, 'Wh…who are you? Bo…both of you…who?'

'That's it?' The European laughed.

The adjutant stork glared at the European before returning his gaze to the scene outside the window.

Rajaram did not answer.

Not that the European gave him any time to answer. Instead, he said, 'I should indeed have introduced ourselves first. I apologize. Let me do it now…. My name is Mephisto.

Plenty of people know me, although you do not.' Pausing, Mephisto added with a mixture of mockery and regret, 'You would have if you'd been to Hindu College.'

Pointing to the adjutant stork, Mephisto continued, 'And this is my companion. His name is Banabehari.'

The bird twisted its neck to throw a glance at Rajaram, as though confirming the announcement.

Rajaram could still find no words. A bizarre scene! And this man with the peculiar name—Mephisto—appeared to know everything about him. And imagine an adjutant stork being named Banabehari!

This was what you called a carnival. Nothing but a carnival.

'Yes, my son, that's it. That's what I'm here for,' said Mephisto.

Rajaram didn't understand. He hadn't spoken, he had only been thinking. The man was a mind reader then.

> Who is he? Is he god? Have I seen god then? But why does god dress in a coat and trousers? God of which country?

'Yes, my son, I can read minds. But I am not god, even though I am very close to him. I am his greatest enemy, rival, foe. His finest adversary.'

Rajaram was consumed by fear and embarrassment simultaneously. His entire body quaked.

'Let me tell you something, Rajaram Deb. But first, be calm. Don't be so fearful. I realize the whole thing is sufficient to induce fear, but look, I'm helpless. This is how we come, this is how we go.'

Silence once more.

Rajaram glanced alternately at Mephisto and Banabehari.

Banabehari, however, didn't turn to look at him at all. Mephisto stared at Rajaram.

'Well, has your fear abated?' Mephisto asked.

Although the answer was no, Rajaram said softly, 'Yes... yes.'

'Very well. Now let me explain the reason for my, that is to say our, visit.'

Suddenly Mephisto turned towards the adjutant stork and berated it, 'And please, Banabehari, there's no need to be so irritated. Just be patient. This is what we do. So please.'

It wasn't as though this admonition had any effect on the bird. It continued to look out the window, as though it had heard nothing.

'Anyway. Never mind. Now listen, Rajaram, to what I have to tell you. We are here because you summoned us....' Mephisto stopped abruptly, as though he was expecting an inevitable question.

Rajaram did not disappoint him, asking the question at once, spontaneously, 'I summoned you? Wha...what do you mean?'

His voice still trembled a little.

'Yes...you summoned us and we came, though I must admit we have been a little late in arriving, which we regret humbly,' said Mephisto, lapsing partly into English.

Rajaram could make no sense of what was going on, and Mephisto switching between Bengali and English compounded the problem. He simply could not comprehend anything, it was all deeply confusing.

'Oh dear, I apologize again. I beg your pardon for speaking in a mixture of Bengali and English. I shall speak only in Bengali from now on. English has infiltrated every language in disguise. Consider my predicament, it isn't even my own language. It bypasses me, bypasses my tongue, can you imagine?'

'I still don't understand.' Rajaram seemed to have got a grip on himself. He was able to speak without stammering.

'Ah, you have regained your voice. Let me explain everything. But first, I must tell you that your cat is a most sweet creature. And you have chosen a beautiful name for her.' Mephisto pointed towards the space below the bed.

Rajaram had nothing to say, Mephisto knew everything. He seemed to be toying with Rajaram. Shedding his apprehension slowly, Rajaram melted slightly and grew a little impatient.

'No, we won't delay things anymore. I...we came because you summoned us. That is to say not called us by our names, since you don't know them. But you called in other ways. For us, that's a call too. Do you know how? Oh, all right, there's no need to be mysterious anymore. I will irk you if I continue to be enigmatic. Listen, then, you have been obsessed with the carnival for such a long time now, you have been shouting the word out loud, or muttering it constantly, it's almost been a decade. So, we couldn't hold ourselves back anymore. We would have been here earlier, but as I said, we were delayed. Inadvertently delayed. I am the carnival, we are the carnival. The carnival is ecstasy, immeasurable ecstasy. Celebrations.'

Mephisto was out of breath after this long speech. He smiled meaningfully after he stopped.

Rajaram listened in amazement. He was not prepared for this wonder. That the word 'carnival' could lead to this situation was beyond his imagination.

Are they ghosts? They're not god. The devil? Spirits?

To Rajaram's astoundment, Banabehari interjected, 'Let me tell you I had absolutely no desire to come here. I don't like being here. It was only to oblige Mephisto. So don't you disrespect us by thinking of us as ghosts.' He sounded enraged. His voice was human but harsh.

Mephisto, who had been watching in silence, spoke up now. 'Enough, kindly stop bickering.' Turning to Rajaram, he said solemnly, 'Now, Rajaram. We are not here to joke with you or have fun…we aren't itinerant jesters. As I told you already, we are here because you summoned us. But once we are here there are some things we must do.'

'I don't understand anything,' Rajaram said, somewhat loudly. His fear was all but gone.

'I…we, are here to make a pact with you,' Mephisto said firmly.

'A pact?'

'Yes, a pact.'

'What pact?'

'A pact to show you the carnival.'

Sensations of excitement, amazement, and wonder seemed to be bursting forth from Rajaram's eyes. How could anyone turn up like this to show him the carnival? Was it even possible? Where would they take him? How would they go?

'All your questions have answers, Rajaram. But first tell us whether you're willing.' Mephisto asked the question knowing full well an answer was unnecessary. Everything was predetermined, after all. But still it was important to ensure the right of choice. A definite yes or a no made a person's perspective clear.

A nonplussed Rajaram didn't know how to respond. He felt a tide of desire to agree with them, but he didn't know what was to follow and how things would unfold.

'We understand, Rajaram, you have doubts, you hesitate. Naturally. We'll give you time to think it over. We'll be back, and by then you must make a decision about your fate. But first let me tell you that we'll take you to see the carnival. You'll find out what the carnival is. We have shown it to many others, we will continue to show it to even more people. But you will have to forsake something in exchange, Rajaram.' The objective was certain to be fulfilled, but Mephisto's speech suggested he still had to deliver an introduction.

'Forsake something? Forsake what?'

'The body. Your body, your sense organs.'

Rajaram shivered. What a horrifying demand! Forsaking the body meant dying. What were they telling him? Would he have to die to see the carnival? Kasiprasad Ghosh had told him the carnival was related to religion.

'The questions that have occurred to you are correct, Rajaram. At the outset, let me tell you I do not accept that the carnival is nothing but a religious matter. The carnival is an exuberance, a passion, a sensation, an ecstasy. There are no laws to limit it, there is no particular period to which it must be confined. The carnival is everywhere, at all levels. An intense, extreme festival. And a festival is not always religious. Everyone sees the carnival one way or another. But yes, although not everyone has to die to see it, some do have to die. For therein lies their liberation. This is the keenest experience of their lives, the highest pinnacle they can climb. Death is the only road to the carnival then. You are one of them, Rajaram. You too have been identified to see the carnival. Yet your route is one of forsaking the body. I will tell you more about this. Not today, however, but when we are here again. And listen, do not tell anyone about our visit or our conversation. All of this is confidential, as you must have realized by now. The truth is that we arrive whether we are summoned or not. The carnival is impossible without us.'

Fear returned to Rajaram. What had he done!

Have I invited my own death? Will I really die? What if I don't see the carnival, what if I don't want to see it?

But no, I will see the carnival. I have to. I have to accomplish something. This is where my liberation lies. Mephisto said so.

'Existence continues even after forsaking the body,' Mephisto declared. 'It's time for a new body then. Think it over, Rajaram, think carefully.'

Rajaram said, almost to his face, 'What is to come? You know very well what is to come.'

Pretending he had not heard, Mephisto did not engage Rajaram on the matter anymore. 'We're late already, we hadn't meant to stay quite so long. You can see how Banabehari has been sulking there all this while with his face turned away. I have to give him some relief too.... Do you miss Krishnabhabini?'

Rajaram was already shattered, and now this question pierced his heart like a bolt of lightning. Why did Mephisto have to ask this?

Rajaram was unable to answer. He only glanced at Mephisto and tried to say, 'You know everything already,' but he could not. But Mephisto broke in to say, 'Aha, I see. There's something I've remembered. This English-to-Bengali dictionary, you're familiar with it, but not with the English one. None of the pages before or after the one with the word carnival is intact.

You must have also realized the pages have been torn out. You have long wished to know how this came to be.'

Mephisto's words opened a fresh vortex of mystery in the already puzzling situation. Faintly Rajaram said, 'Yes, I have. Very much indeed.'

'Very well. I'll relate the incident before I take your leave today. Now listen, the dictionary belonged to your late father. But not exactly to him either. It was actually the property of the magistrate in the village of Bikrampur, where your family once owned an estate. Your father visited this magistrate's office one day on business. The magistrate was not present, and your father decided to wait for him. He happened to pick up the book lying on the desk in front of him. He knew how to read English, and he discovered it was a dictionary written by one Samuel Johnson. He leafed through it for some time, after which the magistrate appeared and they had a conversation. The book remained with your father, who sought permission at the end of the meeting to borrow it for a few days. He was in Bikrampur for some time. You were a boy then. Pleased by your father's request, the magistrate gave him the book as a gift. Although he was embarrassed at first, your father accepted the gift eventually.

'The book accompanied him when he returned to the city. But Rajaram, why was the book ripped apart? That is the most important thing. I'm wondering whether it will be appropriate to tell you these things all these years later.'

Mephisto lapsed into silence. Rajaram was quiet too.

After some thought, Mephisto resumed, 'I might as well tell you. Listen…. Your father had a mistress. Her whereabouts were secret, no one knew except your father's coachman. I will not burden you with details of her name and address.

You can do little with the information. What you must know is that your father had a child with this mistress. Your father's presence at her residence became imperative on the night the birth of the child was imminent. He was informed in secret. Your father went, carrying the dictionary with him. Why, I have not understood even after all these years. Why did he need the dictionary at that moment? It is still incomprehensible to me. Many things do in fact remain incomprehensible no matter who you are. One can assume that he took the book along on a pretext to indicate to everyone at home that everything was quite normal. Many people knew he consulted the book often, they had witnessed him in the act.

'Be that as it may, the lady was wracked with labour pain. Her only maid had fetched a midwife. Your father entered the birthing room directly, catching the midwife unawares. She was pressing down on the lady's abdomen gently with her fingers, and assuring the mother-to-be that the pain would cease shortly. A sheet covered the lady down to her knees.

'When the baby emerged, smeared with blood, the midwife cried out for a soft and clean length of cloth to wrap the infant in.

'"Take that," your father said, pointing to the sheet covering his mistress.

'"Are you mad? Is she supposed to be naked after giving birth? She has to be covered too, do you expect her to put on a sari now?"

'At this your father ran out like a madman in search of a length of cloth. But he could not decide what to bring back. There was nothing suitable, he would have to tear a strip out. But from what? Something occurred to him, and he rushed to this carriage, where he had left the dictionary. He tore out the binding and the opening pages, till the middle of the words beginning with A. And then, choosing at random, the pages from C onwards. Leaving the first few C pages intact, he ripped out the rest and went back inside. He ripped out the pages from the point where the volume ends now. The infant came into the world eventually wrapped in the binding and pages from Dr Johnson's dictionary.

'Much later, the mutilated book, now included among discarded objects, was deposited in the coop below the staircase going up to the roof.'

Mephisto sighed deeply and stopped. He seemed exhausted after narrating this long account.

Learning of the incident could have come as a great shock to Rajaram. He now knew things that were enough to turn many of his assumptions upside down. But after all that had already taken place this evening, the impact of the story he had just heard had plummeted to zero. Or else, after the veil had been lifted on such an explosive piece of family history, it would have been unimaginable for Rajaram to only ask perfunctorily, 'What happened to the child?'

Mephisto grew nervous at this.

'Your father sent mother and child to Benaras. Both are alive.' With this, Mephisto said firmly, so that the conversation could not be prolonged any further, 'We're very late, we'll leave now. We'll be back soon. Though I cannot say when. It might be any day, at any time of day. Take your decision, and be prepared.'

Mephisto moved towards the door. Banabehari followed him, walking past Rajaram with the air of someone who had breathed a sigh of relief.

Rajaram got off his bed gently and followed them with

measured footsteps. Just before leaving, Mephisto said, 'One more thing, your father went there to have his mistress abort the child, but it would not have been possible by then. The mistress had hidden her pregnancy from him for a long time with a futile hope. And don't be afraid, the few other humans that there are in this house are not aware of our arrival. We have purloined their memory for some time, that's all. We have stolen a period of time too, as you will realize shortly.' He smiled. 'We'll go on our way now, but we'll be back, which is when we'll hear your decision and then liberate you. Oh no, I'm using English again. I don't know what comes over me now and then.'

Banabehari had clung to his patience all this while, but now the dam broke at Mephisto's final utterance. 'Enough of your affectations,' he all but shouted, 'I cannot take it anymore.' The bird marched off, overtaking Mephisto, who smiled briefly at Rajaram and followed the adjutant stork without another word.

They disappeared in the wink of an eye. The door remained closed, just as it had been earlier. There was no sign of change.

Rajaram felt himself weighed down by a strange exhaustion. Sleep seemed to be the only solution to this. What had just happened? Why? What next? All such thoughts vanished. He could hear Simantini mewing, she seemed to have become immobile beneath the bed. Rajaram drew her out lightly. She was still staring round-eyed, the haze of surprise had not yet been dispelled.

Kissing her head, Rajaram said, 'Don't be frightened, Simantini, everything is fine.'

Speaking to her reassured him. Setting Simantini down on the bed, he closed the window and lay down next to her. Then he slept, a deep sleep. The clock, however, said it was still evening, its hands having progressed only slightly beyond five past seven.

⁂

After the extraordinary appearance put in by Mephisto and Banabehari, Rajaram's life seemed to have taken a frantic turn. Despite a transitory curiosity about the current fortunes of Debram's mistress and his illegitimate child, he was neither inclined nor interested in reassessing his father in the light of his newly received knowledge. He had become engrossed in introspection. The very foundation of his own stability appeared shaky.

The carnival would take place. It was about to take place. Rajaram would see it. But he would have to surrender himself to them in exchange. Who were they? What species of humans? What was their occupation? They took humans to see the carnival in exchange for their bodies. But then had they not said not everyone had to die to see the carnival? Did those who did not die not see the carnival?

Even as Rajaram wondered and marvelled, he noticed a surprising phenomenon—the more the days passed after the incident, the more his fear dwindled. Things would have to arrive gradually at a culmination for him, it was always on the cards. Perhaps this was the opportunity. His own attitude perturbed him. But the estate? This house? The assets? How were all of these to be settled? Who would look after them?

They had said they would return, and yet Rajaram was unable to arrive at a decision. Nearly a month had passed. What would he tell them if they came suddenly? Today, for instance?

When a few more days had passed, their continued delay threw Rajaram into some doubt. Why such a long interval? Was someone applying black magic?

He had not come to believe in the invisible power, after all.

Consider everything that has taken place. And yet there is no invisible power, you say?

⁓

Nabinmadhab made an appearance one day. He had just had a second son, and was here to invite Rajaram to the formal ceremony of the child's first taste of rice. In course of conversation, he said, 'Have you heard? A soldier named Mangal Pandey fired at a British officer just the other day at the Company's military camp in Barrackpore. The officer escaped providentially. But Pandey's been apprehended. He tried to kill himself before he was arrested, he turned his gun on himself, but he didn't die. Now he will, he'll probably be hanged.'

This was news to Rajaram, it was unprecedented. An Indian had fired at a powerful British officer of the Company. This was the carnival! Would Mangal Pandey see the carnival if he were to be hanged? Was that where Mephisto and Banabehari were?

A few days later Rajaram heard Mangal Pandey was indeed going to be hanged. The rumour had spread everywhere, everyone in the city had come to know. People would even be going to witness the hanging. This was the carnival too—witnessing death. Rajaram recalled his father's description of Maharaj Nandakumar being hanged in public.

⁓

Days passed. There was no sign of Mephisto. Was this some supernatural fraud that had been perpetrated on him? Who were the people responsible for this?

In no time, another summer arrived. A searing summer. On a hot day, when Rajaram had given up hopes of Mephisto's return and was sunk in a siesta, enjoying the comfort of the breeze ensured by the punkah puller, in his sleep he heard someone calling his name close to his ears. It wasn't a completely familiar voice, but not entirely unfamiliar either.

Was he hearing things in his sleep, or was it real? Rajaram could not tell. He was deep in slumber.

A little later there was a warm touch on his ear. But even this didn't wake him up.

A short-lived silence followed.

And then a stentorian yell of 'Rajaram' next to his ears.

He leapt out of his bed in fright, to find Mephisto standing in front of him, and a red-eyed Banabehari behind Mephisto. He grew even more frightened at the sight, and couldn't utter a sound.

'We're here,' said Mephisto with a smile in his voice, as though he had been waiting for this moment.

Banabehari seemed to have been waiting too, but for something else. As soon as Rajaram woke up he said, 'Court jester!' After this, he took up his usual position by the window, which was closed, and ordered Mephisto, 'Who's going to open this? Someone open it.'

Mephisto went towards the window, as though the instructions were not meant for Rajaram at all. As he opened it, he said, 'We didn't make a noise at the door today, I didn't want a noise coming in. Last time it was deliberate. Something so momentous cannot be started in silence. The beginning will remain memorable. The sound, the fear, the wonder.'

From past experience Rajaram knew his apprehensions about anyone else finding out were baseless. As usual, no one would have an inkling about what was going on. They had again stolen time and memories.

Did they steal Simantini's memory too? She had remained frightened for a long time.

Simantini! Where had she gone today? She had been asleep beneath the teapoy. Where was she? Had she crept under the bed? Rajaram couldn't spot her even after bending over to check.

'Simantini's over there, I can see her, she's sitting awkwardly near one of the feet of your bed. In truth, I am making her suffer a little, she can see me, and she can tell nothing of hers has been stolen. She can understand everything, she has kept her real time memory. Because I want her to.'

Although Rajaram wanted to ask why Simantini was being punished, he didn't.

Mephisto was aware of Rajaram's desire to ask this question, but he made no reference to it.

The rays of a declining sun had entered the room. After opening the window, Mephisto stood only a short distance away from Rajaram. Today Rajaram could see him much closer, in a brighter light, and yet Mephisto's face was obscured. Strange! Perhaps it was Mephisto's own magic web.

'What pleasure do you seek from viewing my face, Rajaram?' Mephisto asked lightly. 'Instead tell us what we are here for on this final visit, the reason we exist, the reason you and many others exist. Tell us your decision.'

No sooner had Mephisto stopped than Banabehari exclaimed, slightly louder this time, in his characteristically resentful tone, 'You've been the subject of plays all this while, why don't you start writing your own now? Or act in one yourself. You're so dramatic, honestly.'

Mephisto smiled at this, and then looked questioningly at Rajaram.

No date or time had been fixed for their visit. So this unspecified period of waiting had influenced Rajaram's decision. He had not yet arrived at one. Every day he had told himself he would decide in their presence, every day he had waited for them, and then postponed his decision-making because they had not come. Now that they were actually standing in front of him, Rajaram was nonplussed. Not knowing what to say, he inspected his toes, as though his guardian had caught him about to commit a heinous crime.

'I knew this all along, Rajaram.'

Like a commentator, Banabehari announced, 'There's still time to join the theatre.'

'Please, Banabehari,' said Mephisto in annoyance. 'Shut up.'

Silence reigned for some time.

'I will go, I will see the carnival,' Rajaram declared, breaking the silence.

Mephisto and Rajaram exchanged glances. Rajaram was gazing at Mephisto's face still shrouded in darkness. He was aware that Mephisto was looking at him too, but he could not tell what sort of look it was—twisted, cruel, and sardonic, or dignified, serene, and satisfied.

'Wonderful, so you have answered directly. Very good.' After a pause, Mephisto continued, 'I will tell you the date and time now, the date and time of the carnival.' He then began to pace about the room with the air of someone trying to remember something that was eluding him.

Suddenly stopping at the spot where the letters to Dwarkanath Tagore were kept, he all but leapt in joy and said, 'Eureka! I will tell you a story.'

Rajaram had not yet spoken after conveying his decision to Mephisto. He felt somewhat foolish. What had he gone and said? He had had all the time in the world to think about it, but he had chosen not to. Or had Mephisto tricked him into saying it? To Rajaram, it seemed peculiar that someone who knew so many things without any of them being articulated would wait to hear his decision directly from him. But he had said it anyway. He was face to face with death now. Meanwhile they kept making him the object of their ridicule. Mephisto, for instance, was about to tell him a story.

> What will death be like? My life will leave my body. Will I be aware of it? Will there be pain? Will it hurt? What will it be like, death?

'Calm down, calm down, Rajaram. You will see the carnival, so it isn't death you are face to face with, it's liberation. And trickery? I have always been the living embodiment of subterfuge, Rajaram, after all, I am....' Mephisto stopped halfway. His voice had turned oddly barbaric, a change that Rajaram had detected. He felt a tingle of fear.

> Liberation! Death! Liberation! Death!

'Never mind all that,' Mephisto softened on realizing Rajaram's reaction. 'Let me tell you the story first.'

Rajaram nodded absently.

'Pay attention, all right?' Mephisto began. 'The story is from China, it's very old. There was a botanist there whom everyone called Old Dong. One day his students told him, it is almost time for your great crossing, you should open your enormous vault of knowledge to us now. Old Dong thought it over and realized his students were right. His learning undoubtedly needed an heir. So one day he set out with his students, identifying various plants and trees for them. He informed them of the qualities that each of them possessed, and even asked them to pay their respects to some of the trees. One day, a student pointed to one of the trees and said, you have identified so many plants and trees for us and informed us of their benefits, but you have said nothing about this tall, 2,500-year-old tree.

'Dong appeared somewhat annoyed at this request. It's no use talking about it, he said, there isn't another tree as useless as this one. It gives neither flowers nor fruit, its timber is poor too. This tree is of no use whatsoever.

'That night, the tree appeared in a dream to Old Dong and spoke, all you told your students was that I lack in qualities. But why did you not tell them even once that this is the reason no one has ever taken an axe to me, no one breaks off my branches, and I have lived to be 2,500 years old?

'The story ends here. I hope you have understood the moral and why I told you this story.'

It wasn't as though Rajaram had extracted the deep significance of the tale. Then again, it made no difference whether he answered Mephisto or not, since Mephisto knew everything anyway. Still, he said, 'Yes.'

Mephisto seemed to ignore the truth even though he knew what it was. Delighted at Rajaram's response, he said, 'Splendid! I knew I would make you understand.'

A little later he continued, 'Inertness is life too, Rajaram. The inert also inhale and exhale. They too wait for a conclusion, and it does come to them. The carnival takes place, I show it to them. Even within the animate there exists the inanimate. What binds them? The inert are actually the most animate. Denying inertness will turn the mobile into the immobile.

There is a carnival of success, and there is a carnival of failure. Those who are successful will see the carnival of success, and those who have failed will see the carnival of failure. But the carnival is inevitable.'

Even though Rajaram did not understand the sum and substance of what Mephisto had said, he seemed to have been given sublime inspiration from the tale. His features were suddenly suffused by brightness.

Mephisto had walked away to the distant corner of the room while talking. Now he whirled abruptly, sat down on Rajaram's teapoy, and began speaking as though hypnotized, 'Monday, the twenty-second day in the month of Ashadh. The commencement of day, which means the appointed hour will be at dawn. It will begin then. Two of my trusted associates, Rosencrantz and Guildenstern, will be here to escort you. We will not fetch you ourselves, although we will meet, of course. Keep the windows closed and the slats raised. Keep the door closed too. But don't lock any of them. They will take you, and I will be present to greet you. So will Banabehari. And then we will proceed with you. The carnival will begin.'

Rajaram listened in wonder. Every cell in his body was charged with excitement.

The carnival! The carnival!

'And listen, Rajaram. Sever all ties, all ties.'

The words resounded at once in Rajaram's ears. 'Sever all ties.'

Mephisto had risen from the teapoy now. Banabehari, who had been silent all this while, followed suit and fluttered his wings two times. Pleased that the mission was complete, he prepared to leave.

Suddenly, and for no obvious reason, an entirely unrelated question occurred to Rajaram. He had no idea why it had come up in his head right now. 'Since you know everything, you must also have come to know I have dreams. Strange dreams. But they all have something in common, there's blood in all of them. Why so much blood?'

'I know, Rajaram. And your question is pointless, because its answer has not been constructed yet. Many in the future will ask this question. The answer will be available after it's asked for the last time. The last one to ask it will be given the answer.'

Which world was he talking of? Was it a world outside this one? Or was there another world in parallel to this one? Rajaram found himself pinned down by arrows of perplexity.

'You will understand everything slowly, Rajaram. We will take our leave at once. Be prepared. Monday, the twenty-second day of Ashadh. One more celebration is scheduled on that particular day, there will be a carnival in this city too. A carnival of new lights.'

They vanished in moments. In the empty room, Rajaram gazed in surprise at the void.

A little later a mewing was heard.

∽

Rajaram experienced no relief after Mephisto and Banabehari's final departure. He was anxious and constantly impatient. Death did not frighten him, he felt no fear even after knowing his last day in the manifested world had been finalized, he was not afraid although this day was approaching. He was surprised himself. What death, it was a carnival. No, not death. Never.

And so he awaited the day with excitement. Mephisto's associates would be here to escort him. Who were they? What would they be like? Their names were tongue-twisters too.

After Mephisto and Banabehari left, Rajaram performed two tasks with great wisdom and swiftness. The first was to ask an astrologer he knew, Anadi Siddhantabagish, to determine the accurate time of sunrise on the twenty-second day of Ashadh, 6 July 1857 according to the English calendar. And the second was more important, which was to prepare a will. In his father's absence he was the owner of all the moveable and immoveable assets of the family, the responsibility for all future decisions was his. Therefore, he was the one who had to prepare a new will.

The person who had prepared Rajaram's father's will was dead. He had sent for Nabinmadhab, considering it unnecessary to consult a different lawyer. Still, he had thought it over briefly. A neighbour would now have all the inside information. Would it be right to reveal so much to Nabinmadhab? But Rajaram would in fact be able to tell him a great deal if he trusted him. After all, Nabin and he knew each other well. So, it was him that Rajaram had sent for finally, even though he did have some concerns. Since Nabinmadhab had known him a long time, what if he questioned Rajaram about his decisions in the will? What if he wanted to know more? What then? And even if he didn't go so far, if he merely asked why Rajaram wanted to compose a will at this age, since he was far from old, what would be Rajaram's answer? Moreover, what would Nabinmadhab's attitude towards Rajaram's heir be like?

'Simantini!'

'Yes, Nabinmadhab, Simantini will be the heir, or rather heiress, to all my moveable and immoveable property. I have taken a final decision on this subject, please do not assume it was an impulsive one. I have thought about it carefully. You may think I have taken leave of my senses, but no matter what your impression might be, Simantini is indeed my heiress. If she has children, they will inherit everything from her. And only in their absence will this building be demolished and all the wealth distributed among the poor.'

'But, an animal...how....'

'It can be done. If it is done, it will be possible. She will own everything. Humans will look after it all. This will make it possible.'

Nabinmadhab did not prolong the conversation. Here to draft a will, he was truly bewildered. And so dumbstruck that he asked none of the questions Rajaram had expected. Even when Rajaram said, 'I am giving you the responsibility for paying all my employees in my absence from the money I will leave behind,' he was quite annoyed at this burden on him, but he neither asked any personal questions, nor objected to anything. He appeared not to have emerged from the fog of surprise he had been plunged into.

The appointed hour kept getting closer. Rajaram felt every intervening day was taking much longer to come to an end. He tried to condense the hours by sleeping and by any other means he could think of. Although Latu and Shashi had noticed certain changes in Rajaram's routine, they had not dared bring these up. They had witnessed a great deal, so even when they observed such things, they were no longer surprised.

Things were not going well in the city and the country.

Mangal Pandey's act of firing a gun and his subsequent hanging had changed many things in national politics. Other parts of the country had been affected too. All kinds of news were being passed around—the white officers were terrified of being attacked by Mangal Pandey's companions. One day, it was rumoured that all the water tanks in the city would be filled with forbidden meat. On another day the word spread that Pandey's fellow soldiers had left their camp in Barrackpore and gone on a rampage, looting had begun, the Britishers were fleeing in fear. There was considerable activity in the city. Columns of the Company's soldiers marched at night through the neighbourhoods where the locals lived.

Rajaram had only one concern—what if the carnival were disrupted? There were only a few days to go.

During the last few days, he felt his faith being eroded. He kept feeling he had launched himself on the winds of fancy, that nothing would actually take place on the that fated day of Ashadh. Should he not have got more details? He should have gathered his courage and put everything to the test. He didn't really know yet what was to happen, did he?

Rajaram now felt it was all a lie, that he was the innocent victim of a fraudulent supernatural conspiracy to keep him immersed in a curious and expectant state of mind.

But at times he found himself wishing this were indeed the case.

The very next moment he recollected Mephisto's instruction—sever all ties. Rajaram had done just that, he had been self-assured and resolute in this regard. Even when he felt a twinge of weakness, he had gathered himself with firmness.

To Rajaram, the twenty-first day of Ashadh was a source of unnecessary delay on his way to the twenty-second. He spent most of the day sleeping, not even eating in the afternoon. For some time, a thought flowed through his mind—tomorrow at this hour he would not be at home, he would not be breathing this air or experiencing this smell and touch he knew so well, this familiar feeling would not be around him. He would no longer have to count out the seventeen steps he took from the bed to the door, the fifteen from the door to the staircase leading to the roof, or the twenty to the one taking him downstairs. He could walk around this house blindfolded. Tomorrow he would depart from this home that he had known since birth, that had seeped into his pores, to see the carnival.

Despite this, the day offered no special dimension or significance to Rajaram. The twenty-first was a day just like any other.

> The death they are talking of surely cannot be a literal death. How can I see anything if I am dead? A consciousness of some kind is bound to persist. It cannot exactly be death.

The only thing Rajaram had done was to ask for some hilsa to be made for his meal at night. The hilsa in monsoon was his favourite fish. Biting into the hilsa that night, Rajaram realized for the first time that he was a passenger now. A passenger-in-waiting.

> The carnival! The carnival!

After his meal the words emerged suddenly through Rajaram's lips, 'He severed the heads of Ravan, not one but ten. But with the creator's boon they sprouted again.'

Swiftly rinsing his hands and mouth, Rajaram undressed and lay down on his bed.

Sever all ties.

Where would the carnival take place? Rajaram didn't know. Nor did he have any idea where Mephisto and Banabehari would take him, or what the carnival would comprise. He would see immeasurable ecstasy, intense celebrations. But who would be experiencing these? He didn't know. What was Rajaram's role? He didn't know. It was through this enormous ignorance that he would enter the orbit of knowledge.

Without giving a reason, Rajaram asked for Simantini not to be served as much food as usual that night. He gave instructions for a bowl of milk to be put in his room for her. Shortly before midnight, Rajaram took the lid off the bowl and offered the milk to Simantini. The objective was not to let her sleep. She was Rajaram's heiress, she simply had to be awake. She would be the only living witness whose memory or time would not be stolen.

Simantini drank the milk. After disrobing, a completely naked Rajaram lay on his bed under a sheet, gazing at her. Occasionally his eyes shifted to the door and windows. As instructed, both were closed but not locked, and the window slats were raised.

Rajaram had no idea who would visit him and which way they would come.

The fan hanging overhead was silent today, as though confronted by the end. Rajaram had paid the punkah puller Gayaram his full salary and asked him to leave two days ago. Gayaram had no idea though that this was his final assignment here.

The lamps remained lit all night.

Everyone had heard that the city would get gas lights for the first time the next day. In Chowringhee. Looking at the light of the lamp, Rajaram remembered two other things: Chandramadhab telling him, 'Our black town, Rajaram, will become even blacker, it will get much darker here' and Mephisto saying, 'There will be a carnival in this city too. A carnival of new lights.' Rajaram would not have the opportunity to see the new lights in the city.

Or will I?

Propping up his pillow, Rajaram sat up with his back against it, running his eyes across his room, the furniture, and everything else in it.

> Is it more pleasurable to bid farewell in familiar surroundings? It must be heart-breaking to say goodbye somewhere unknown, all the while filled with the desire to return to a familiar place.

Simantini stretched her legs out and lay down after finishing her milk. Let her, let her lie down for a while. But he would have to rouse her at the right time. Rajaram found himself glancing at her repeatedly.

He had also decided to stay up all night, although it was not a usual practice. Sleep may have come late to him sometimes, but he had never actually passed an entire night without sleep. This was his first night-long vigil. And so, a drowsiness wrapped its arms lightly around him without his realizing it. His eyes began to close. He leaned forward. The sheet covering him shifted.

The night was almost spent. The lamplight held signs of an

end. A cold and wondrous breeze, redolent with the fragrance of ittar, had just begun to blow in through the open window slats.

SEVEN

The appointed hour of dawn.
The first light filtered in through the window slats. Birdsong could be heard.

So, the carnival was due to begin anytime now.

Rajaram ran to the window. When he opened them, he could see the sky growing light. He gazed at it. A reddish sky, the crimson hue spreading all over it slowly. The sun, round, shimmering. The gentle glow of the first sunbeams fell on Rajaram's face and eyes. He didn't need water, the rays could wash his face clean. Why had he not done this ever before?

He was viewing a sunrise such as this one for the first time. In his heart there was remorse, in his body he felt an acute excitement. 'He severed the heads of Ravan, not one but ten.'

Rajaram stood there for some time, not moving from his position. Suddenly he became alert to the fact that the cold breeze with the scent of ittar had disappeared completely. What he could smell now was incense, the kind of fragrance encountered on entering a temple. Rajaram could not identify its source. Were Latu or Shashi up already? Should he open the door a crack and see for himself?

Closing the window again, Rajaram turned around and almost jumped out of his skin.

A pair of dwarfish, dark-skinned men were standing silently. Dressed like the adivasis of the country, they seemed to have been here for a while, waiting for Rajaram to turn away from the window.

The door was closed, as it had been earlier, as though it had not even been touched.

So all of them had astral bodies.

Even though he was startled, Rajaram had no trouble identifying them. They had to be Mephisto's associates, who were supposed to escort him. He no longer remembered their names, which were tongue-twisters.

Oh, the tricks the man has been up to!

The light coming into the room disappeared suddenly, as though a lamp had gone out abruptly. Turning towards the window again, Rajaram was astonished to see it was now open. Some unknown magic had, in the blink of an eye, turned the same sky that had been filled with a bright crimson glow moments ago completely black.

The two dwarfs were probably mute. They hadn't uttered a single word yet, only staring stonily at Rajaram.

Simantini was awake. How strange! Instead of being frightened, she sat on the bed, observing the two diminutive strangers with sharp eyes.

Therefore, it was time. The journey must begin.

But how should Rajaram dress?

Oho, he hadn't thought of asking. And they hadn't told him either.

But why had he not chosen what to wear in all these days? In all this time? Was he waiting for certainty? There was no time to think of any of this now. He would have to leave at once.

He only had a shawl wrapped around himself. Could he possibly see the carnival dressed in nothing more than a shawl?

No, he would have to dress properly. But would these two keep standing here in front of him? How long would they wait? Even though it wouldn't take him long to dress, would they give him enough time? Or would they insist he go with them dressed as he was now.

Rajaram asked the dwarfs.

They were silent, staring at Rajaram as before. Were they deaf too?

Although no answer was forthcoming, Rajaram decided he would not leave till he had dressed in elegant clothes. Even if they couldn't hear him and would not respond, Rajaram informed them of this. 'Look, I don't know whether you can hear me. Or, even if you do, whether you can speak or not. In any event, I am going to change these clothes, I will dress in a different set of garments.'

He pointed at his shawl, so that their visual sense might help them understand him at least partly. He was also in doubt about the level of respect he should accord them when addressing them—were they superior to him, equals, or inferior? Eventually he chose to think of them as equals.

> Respect for Mephisto, but disdain for them because they
> are only his associates. Is this right? Never mind.

They remained silent, not even a muscle on their faces twitched. Sometimes they appeared to be flesh and blood statues. Lifeless. All they did was stand and stare.

But how could Rajaram dress with them looking on?

What option did he have? He would have to do it this way. They hadn't said a word.

Rajaram was quite embarrassed at the idea of being completely naked in their presence. And all they did was to gape.

Anyway, no point wasting time. Rajaram took his shawl off and put it on the floor. And noticed the dwarfs turning around to face the door.

Marvellous, reflected Rajaram. The carnival!

He got dressed very quickly, and went up to the mirror with the final piece of apparel, his turban. There was a damp darkness all around, amidst which he looked at himself. His image in the mirror was indistinct, as though he would melt any moment. Like wax. Rajaram thrust his face towards the mirror, touching the glass with his forehead. It was cold. He was looking himself in the eye now. He gazed at himself, placing his palms on the mirror, one on each side.

Suddenly he was afraid. In the mirror he saw dark lines beneath his eyes. Sunken.

Whose eyes are those?

He sprang back from the mirror. No need to stand here anymore.

Sever all ties.

Rajaram applied ittar generously on his neck, next to his ears, and on his wrists. Its scent mingled with the fragrance. The room had filled with the fragrance of incense earlier, now a peculiar new smell was born with the scent of ittar added to it.

Simantini was still seated on the bed. All signs of fear had disappeared from her expression. She wasn't even mewing today.

Going up to her, Rajaram held out his arms and took her in them. He planted a long kiss on her head, between her ears.

'Do as I ask you to, all right? You won't have any trouble

here. You will sleep on this bed from now on. I'm leaving now, I'm going to see the carnival.'

After one more kiss, Rajaram put her back on the bed.

Then, addressing Mephisto's associates, who were standing with their back to him, he said, 'Let us go, I am ready.'

They turned around at once, and then marched towards the door. Rajaram followed them. They barely came up to his knees. Even at this hour of his life, Rajaram was amused. The dwarfs opened the door with their hands. Simantini had jumped down from the bed to lap up the milk from the half-covered bowl. She watched round-eyed as the three asymmetrical creatures disappeared gradually. A gust of wind slammed the door shut after they left.

The veranda.

As soon as Rajaram stepped across the threshold of the room and set his foot outside, the drumming began. The kind of drumming that could be heard while the goddess Durga was worshipped. But oh, this was the dream he used to have, wasn't it? Yes, it was identical. The same overcast sky, the same sound of drums. Just like he had seen in his dreams. Was... was this a dream too, then? Rajaram trembled.

Today he didn't dare lean over the balustrade like he did in his dream. He had heard the door to his room slam, but he couldn't bring himself to look back. He moved ahead. The drumming was getting louder. It was clear that there were not hundreds but thousands of drummers. The spaces that Rajaram left behind as he walked were instantly taken over by drummers.

Flanked by the dwarfs, Rajaram descended the stairs towards the thakurdalan.

The sound of conch shells began.

Rajaram had goose pimples, his insides heaved. No, he wasn't dreaming, all of this was indeed taking place before his eyes. In his own home. Where were Latu and Shashi then? Had time been stolen, had memories been robbed? He hadn't met them in the dreams either. Couldn't the neighbours hear the din? What about Nafar and the coachman outside? What were they all thinking? Had everyone's memories and time been plundered? Rajaram was certain no one would find out about Mephisto's exploits, but he had not expected this crescendo of noise and elaborate arrangement in reality. Were these festivities inaudible to everyone? What if they came into the house to see what was going on? How would the secrecy be protected?

But at the same time, it occurred to Rajaram that he was only a traveller now, nothing but a spectator. His journey and his viewing were predetermined, and the responsibility for it had been entrusted to someone else. Which was why the questions, all the questions, became irrelevant as soon as they were born. In a flash. He was above everything at the moment.

Around Rajaram innumerable unknown young and middle-aged women blew on their conch shells. They were dressed in white saris with red borders. Their hair was wet and untied. They wore vermilion in the partings in their hair, their soles were outlined with red dye. On their wrists were gold jewellery and the traditional shell bangles worn by married women. Giant gold necklaces hung around their necks. Their faces were coated a dazzling white. They blew on their conch shells. as though in a trance, completely oblivious to Rajaram's and the two dwarfs' presence.

Rajaram went down to the thakurdalan and stopped. Rows of drummers on either side of him were beating their drums like madmen. Their faces were also white like those of clowns. The corners of their eyes had been elongated by lines of paint stretching to their ears. Silky white bird feathers fluttered like flags from the edges of their drums.

The women were blowing their conch shells to match the rhythm of the drummers' beats. When the beats became faster, so did the conch shells. As though there was stiff competition between the two sets of musicians.

Rajaram walked through their ranks to the edge of the courtyard. More surprises awaited him here. A magical scene had been wrought.

The entire courtyard was filled with red water. On it were scattered hundreds of red hibiscus flowers, floating on the surface. A large number of men were standing in this pool, immersed up to their waists. Their bodies were bare. Their foreheads were streaked with lines of sandalwood paste. Enormous rings hung from their ears. Holding clay pots of incense, they danced intently. There in the pool, they danced, the smoke from the incense covering the sky. The air was saturated with the smell of burning incense.

Whom do they worship? Is this actually worship?

The clouds were lit by snaking lines of lightning. Claps of thunder could be heard at intervals. It had begun to pour. Raindrops fell on the water gathered in the courtyard, on the bodies of the men holding pots of incense, on the petals of the floating red hibiscus flowers. There were so many flowers that even if one of them sank beneath the weight of the water, another one surfaced immediately.

The incense burnt. The drummers began to dance. First one, then another, then a few more followed suit. Eventually, all of them. Everyone danced.

Suddenly Rajaram felt the touch of a hand on his shoulder. Swivelling his head, he discovered it was Mephisto. Today, too, his face was obscured in shadows. Behind him, with an expression of serenity today, stood Banabehari.

'How does it feel, Rajaram? Welcome to the inauguration of the carnival. Now Banabehari and I will take you to the main segment. I hope my courtiers escorted you here properly.'

Rajaram was aware that he had not turned numb, as he usually did in his dreams.

'I am enjoying myself. Yes, they escorted me properly. I'm ready, let's go.'

'Very well.'

Looking around, Rajaram saw the dwarfs had disappeared. Mephisto was on his right now, and Banabehari on his left.

'We will enter this pool of water slowly, Rajaram,' said Mephisto and climbed one step down towards the courtyard. So did Banabehari.

Rajaram followed them like one of the faithful.

Like the floating hibiscuses, the rows of men with the incense pots parted to make way for the three of them as they entered the water. Rajaram's eyes smarted, the sting of the burning incense making them water. Red hibiscuses, sodden with red water, adhered to his clothes. Raindrops fell on him, dislodging the flowers from his body and making them drop back in the red water.

'Stop here. Look around you,' said Mephisto.

Startled, Rajaram saw gigantic sheets of cloth fall like screens on all sides of his house. The very next moment images appeared on these screens. Not still but moving. Pictures that moved. Bright, colourful.

This was an image of the city. A moving image. How huge everything was, the bodies of the people and their faces too. The images showed them going about their daily work, some at home, some outside.

Can they not tell they are on display?

Mephisto pointed to one of the screens. 'Look at that one,' he told Rajaram.

It was Chowringhee, Rajaram saw. Lights shone on posts with designs etched into them.

'Gas lights,' said Mephisto.

Gas lights! Oh! So incredibly bright! The road was lit up. White men and women were strolling about. So many different kinds of carriages! Everything looked new under this new illumination, utterly novel. Rajaram had been to Chowringhee before, several times, but these lights had transformed everything in an instant. Lights change so many things.

Lowering his eyes from this astonishing sight, Rajaram saw another extraordinary scene. The men who were drumming and the women who were blowing on their conch shells had moved to the sides of the terrace, and their place had been taken by some naked men and women with purple bodies. They were copulating furiously, screaming like beasts.

'Surprise is an element of the carnival, Rajaram, surprise waits here for an audience.' Turning towards Mephisto when he spoke, what Rajaram saw was a horrifying illustration of his words.

In the middle of the pool of red water stood Krishnabhabini, her pose suggesting she had just surfaced. On either side of her, the men were engrossed in dancing with their incense pots. Through the smoke and incessant rain Krishnabhabini could be seen to be completely naked. Red hibiscuses clung to various parts of her body as though they had bloomed there. The rain made some of them drop into the water.

Krishnabhabini's body had taken on the red hue of coloured powder. Her long hair cascaded down her back.

Her eyes were fixed on Rajaram.

He was petrified. What did these people want to do with him? Had the soul returned in bodily form?

'Come, Rajaram,' Mephisto said.

Rajaram didn't move.

He gaped at Krishnabhabini, fear written all over on his face. What was Krishnabhabini going to do to him?

> Why did you come back this way, Bini? Why did you return? I saw you in the dream too. And again today. Right in front of me, in this manner. This isn't a dream, this is no dream.

Since Rajaram hadn't budged, Mephisto said, 'What's the matter, Rajaram? Move.'

Still Rajaram couldn't move, he felt paralysed. Now Krishnabhabini—or was it Krishnabhabini's body—advanced towards him. All this while she was immersed up to her navel, now the nether part of her body became visible slowly.

Krishnabhabini rose out of the water in Rajaram's direction.

'Come on Rajaram, move!' Mephisto began to lead him away by the hand. Banabehari started moving the hibiscus flowers with his beak for no good reason.

Krishnabhabini and Rajaram were face to face now. Both were wet, the water dripping slowly from their bodies. Their eyes were fixed on each other's. Krishnabhabini's reddened skin seemed to be growing lustrous at the touch of the raindrops. The raindrops bounced off both of them in combined exuberance, splashing on their faces as though determined to exchange places. The scent of their rain-soaked bodies was mixed with the raindrops now, their senses were submerged in it. There were thunderclaps in the sky. The screens hanging around the building flapped noisily in the gusty wind. The rain became more intense. Miraculously, this had no effect on the burning incense, from which the smoke continued to rise as before. The men kept dancing in the same rhythm with their torsos bared. The drummers raised their pitch. The drumbeats became louder. Conch shells were blown. Now some of the women ululated. Amidst the various sounds and musical notes, a gigantic current of blood-red water that had taken birth surreptitiously, without anyone noticing, crashed like an oceanic wave with tremendous force over everyone. A violent flood ensued, maddened torrents of water. A storm. The array of sounds was disrupted and fragmented. Countless human voices were heard, weeping and pleading, as though struggling desperately to stay afloat, to survive. But they couldn't save themselves from drowning. They sank, all of them sank. At the moment of sinking, they turned red, as though with remorse at the fact that while they were engaged in their lascivious acts, they had not realized, not remotely imagined, that they would lose their lives this way just a few moments later. Cries of contrition could be heard, mingled with pleas. All the sounds and musical notes disappeared under wails of desperation. The tyranny of the water made escape impossible.

Then. Silence.

Everything was completely soundless. As though someone who had been generating all the noise had shut everything off.

Only the uncontrollably cascading water could be heard. The sound of water. And thereafter, sounds of serial explosions all around. Sounds of crumbling. Sounds of destruction.

Everything fell to pieces. The building collapsed. Land and water became one. The sky came down to the earth. The earth rose to the sky.

A chugging could be heard, smoke could be seen rising. It was being expelled continuously from something that resembled a small tube. The tube was set on a moving object shaped like a rolling pin. A metallic vehicle. Several wheels turned at a fantastic speed beneath the vehicle. The wondrous cart of metal advanced through the ruins. A train. Long, snake-like. With mighty force, the train sped forward.

The carnival!

The carnival had begun.

'What you are seeing is the carnival, Rajaram Deb. The carnival. You are the man in the myth now.'

'I am the man in the myth. I am the man in the myth. I am seeing the carnival. Ram Ravan Christ Mephisto. Ram Ravan Christ Mephisto. I am Ram I am Ravan I am Christ I am Mephisto. I...I am the man in the myth.'

You are the only voyager in the heavens, o sun, you control all. Surya, son of Prajapati, draw back your beams, your dazzling light, so that I may see your glory, I am the one within you.

EIGHT

The door opened at the lightest of touches. The day was well advanced by now.

Rajaram lay on the bed. No animation in his body. It was cold as ice. He was naked. Sunlight streamed in through the open window and fell on him, giving his hair a golden hue. His hands were on his chest, arranged as though in prayer. His legs were straight, stretched out. His eyes were closed, and a wonderful serenity marked his face. His body gave off the fragrance of ittar.

Was this how Rajaram had been lying? Like a corpse? How did death's tryst with him take place?

It was impossible to tell. There were no signs on the body—no injury or wound. Rajaram's naked, lifeless death appeared to have been laid out with great care.

Who did it? Who arranged his body this way? How did death occur? It was impossible to tell. No one ever found out.

The first to see Rajaram's dead body, to touch it, was Latu. Oh, the wonder in his eyes!

One by one they arrived, everyone who was supposed to come in such an eventuality.

Simantini could not be found. She was never found. The entire house, every corner, was searched, even other houses in the neighbourhood. But nothing. Simantini had vanished.

In the evening Rajaram's funeral procession left the house.

Only a handful of people accompanied the body.

On the road, a group of dancing girls chanted, 'Babu has died, Babu has died,' and defying the efforts made by Latu, Nafar, and Nabinmadhab—the last-named among them from his own carriage—forced themselves into the procession with the choicest expletives. Their intent was unknown, and they left just before reaching the crematorium.

That same evening, the first gas lights went on in Chowringhee, home to the British.

A carnival. A carnival of new light.

Notes

Ashadh

Ashadh is the fourth month according to the Hindu calendar, running from mid-June to mid-July; a period of heavy rain in Bengal.

Bhoot Chaturdashi

Celebrated on the fourteenth day (Chaturdashi) of the lunar month of Kartik (the eighth month according to the Hindu calendar, running from mid-October to mid-November), Bhoot Chaturdashi is a day of abolishing or warding off evil by lighting lamps. Usually, it is the day before Kali Puja.

Durga Puja

The major religious festival of the Bengali-speaking community, Durga Puja is held every autumn. It is a spectacular worship of the Goddess Durga, conducted both in homes and as a community effort.

Kali Puja

Kali Puja is the annual ceremony of the worship of Goddess Kali, held in autumn.

Kashiram Das

One of the most important poets of medieval Bengal, Kashiram Das lived in approximately the first half of the seventeenth century. He translated the Mahabharata into Bengali in verse, though scholars argue that only the first four books or 'parvas' were his translation. These four parvas were first published by the Serampore Mission Press, between 1801 and 1803.

Kobial
The instant poets or minstrels of nineteenth-century Bengal, kobials often performed live and engaged in poetic/singing duels known as 'Kobir Lorai' or 'Fight of the Poets'.

Panchali, Half-akhrai, and Dhop
These are all genres and forms of popular music and entertainment in nineteenth-century Bengal. While panchali refers to an oral narrative song, half-akhrai is a trendy folk song (mostly about love and lovers) originating from the Vaishnav akharas or institutions. Dhop is a musical tradition hailing from the Vaishnav Kirtan cult.

Punkah puller
The domestic member of staff who operated the punkah or fan in colonial times, using a string and pulley system.

Ramnidhi Gupta (1741–1839)
Singer, song-writer, and more famously known as Nidhu Babu, Ramnidhi Gupta is one of the best exponents of tappa songs and music in nineteenth-century Bengal. He was also one of the very first writers of patriotic songs in Bengali.

Rupchand Pakshi (1815–1890)
Also known as Rupchand Das Mahapatra, Rupchand Pakshi is a native bard and singer, whose satirical lyrics centred around contemporary personalities and affairs. His songs incorporated an idiosyncratic blend of English and Bengali. Curiously, his group or band of singers named themselves after various birds, which earned them their title, 'Pakshir Dal' or 'The Band of Birds'.

Serampore Mission Press
A legacy of the Danish and British colonial era, the press in Serampore (now Srirampore), Bengal, was founded in 1800 by British Baptist missionaries, chief among them being William Carey and William Ward. The press was operational till 1837, and published major linguistic, cultural, and religious texts in Bengali and other languages. The first Bengali newspaper and magazine too was published by the press.

Shoima
Shoi in Bengali means friend, and ma is mother. Shoima is a portmanteau word for the accepted, non-biological relationship of godmother.

Tappa
Originally the folk songs of camel riders in Punjab, the tappa was a popular form of music in nineteenth-century Bengal. From the subalterns to the elites, the tappa found admirers and patrons among all classes.

Thakurdalan
This refers to a large expanse of space in old Bengali mansions where deities are installed and religious rituals are performed.

Vaidya
Usually a practitioner of Ayurvedic medicine, the word also referred generally to doctors.

'You are the only voyager in the heavens, o sun, you control all. Surya, son of Prajapati, draw back your beams, your dazzling light, so that I may see your glory, I am the one within you.'

—The sixteenth sloka or verse of the Ishapanishad